This Book
Belongs To:

Book II
of the Agnes Kelly
Mystery Adventure Series

Book I
Intrigue in Istanbul

Book III
All is Revealed in Russia

Also by
Christine Keleny

For All Ages
The Red Velvet Box

Chakra Magic

For Adults
Rosebloom
A Burnished Rose
Rose from the Ashes

Living in the House of Drugs

*Will the Real Carolyn Keene
Please Stand Up*

Narrow Escape in Norway

Book II

Christine Keleny

CKBooks

Contact Christine Keleny and see all of her books at: christinekelenybooks.com

Publisher's Cataloging-In-Publication Data

Names: Keleny, Christine.
Title: Narrow escape in Norway / Christine Keleny.
Description: New Glarus, WI : CKBooks, [2017] | Series: An Agnes Kelly mystery adventure ; book II | Interest age level: 009-016. | Summary: "Book II in the Agnes Kelly series takes Agnes and her grandmother to Norway in their continuing quest to find out what happened to Agnes' father (and Grandmother Agee's son). They have new adventures and find themselves in dangerous circumstances."--Provided by publisher.
Identifiers: LCCN 2017942171 | ISBN 978-1-949085-06-8 | ISBN 978-0-9892152-7-5 (ebook) | ISBN 978-0-9892152-6-8 (hardcover)
Subjects: LCSH: Girls--Travel--Norway--Juvenile fiction. | Grandparent and child--Juvenile fiction. | Fathers--Death--Juvenile fiction. | Intelligence service--Norway--Juvenile fiction. | Intelligence service--United States--Juvenile fiction. | CYAC: Girls--Travel--Norway--Fiction. | Grandparent and child--Fiction. | Fathers--Death--Fiction. | Intelligence service--Norway--Fiction. | Intelligence service--United States--Fiction. | LCGFT: Detective and mystery fiction. | Action and adventure fiction.
Classification: LCC PZ7.1.K45 Na 2017 (print) | LCC PZ7.1.K45 (ebook) | DDC [Fic]--dc23

Published by CKBooks Publishing
PO Box 214
New Glarus, WI 53574
ckbookspublishing.com

Font used courtesy of Lee Batchelor: "5th Grade Cursive"

To my best childhood friend,
creator of codes and fellow
Pig Latin speaker:
Tracy
a.k.a. Crazy Bee

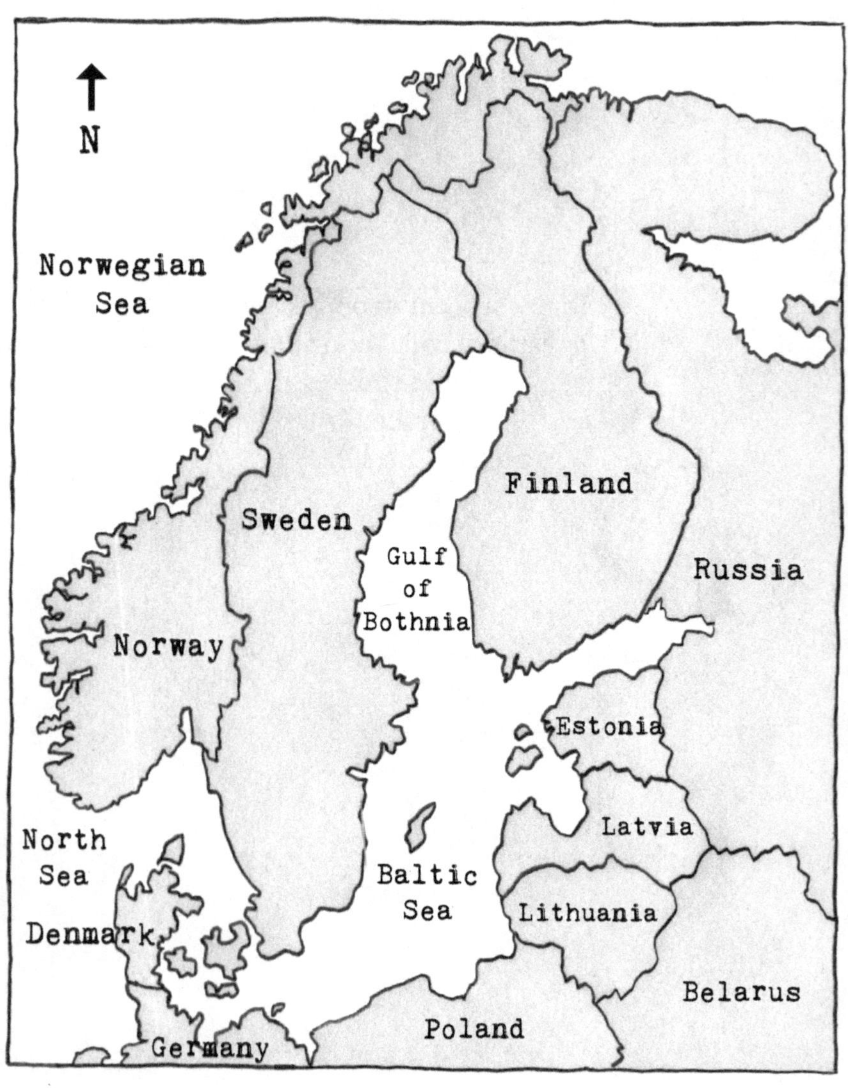

Agnes' Map of Scandinava

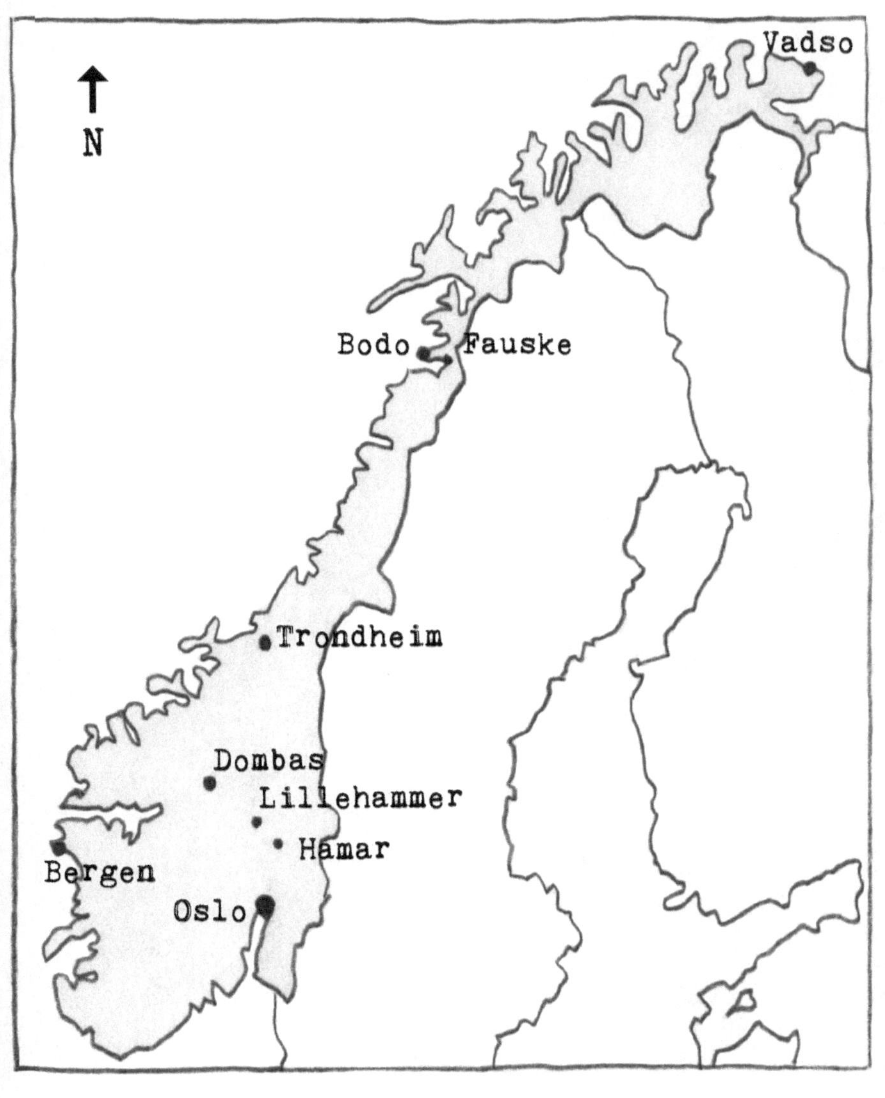

Agnes' Map of Norway

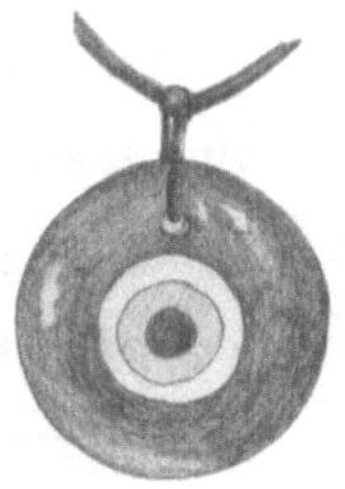

Chapter One

I pick up the flat, round, glass evil-eye pendant that's sitting around my neck, next to my dead dad's Saint Christopher medal, and I rub it between my fingers as I think about what to put in my letter to my best friend. She's not going to believe what happened and what I found out, but I have to tell someone.

Dear Peggy,

I hardly know where to start. I told you about Yusuf in that postcard I sent you of the Blue Mosque. (Pretty cool place, don't you think? It's even more impressive in person.) What I didn't tell you was that Yusuf helped me find out why

Grandma Agee wanted to go to Istanbul. It wasn't just a random [adj: chosen or done without a particular plan or pattern] place she wanted to visit. You better sit down for this next part.

Apparently, my dad died under what my grandmother described as "suspicious" circumstances! But that's not the half of it. Remember when I told you he worked for the government selling insurance? Well, he was just pulling the wool over our eyes. That's one of those idioms I told you about. It means he was telling us one thing but something entirely different was true. He worked for the government, all right, but he worked for the ◆✓❀, which stands for the ◆▱⊏=↷❀⑥ ✓⊏=⑥⑥✓↔▱⊏◆▱ ❀↔▱⊏◆%. [Note: Since my dad worked for the ◆✓❀, I thought we should start using the cipher we came up with when we were ten, so no one will be able to read the secret part of our notes to each other. My cipher key is inside my Agatha Christie book "Murder on the Orient Express" if you can't find yours.] And he wasn't selling insurance, he worked in ▱☺△✓★⊏❀↔▱. That's a new word grandma taught me. It means he was a ☺△%! Yup, just like Charlie Chan in that movie we saw on TV with Adam (It was late when we were watching it, and I think you fell asleep and missed most of it so you might not remember it.)

I'm not Charlie Chan, of course, but I kind of feel like him. Grandma wants to find out what happened to my dad, and I promised to help (How cool is that!), so we aren't coming home when we thought we were.

I don't know if you noticed, but this letter has a postmark from Paris (at least I hope it will). We're heading to Paris from Istanbul. Then we hop on a plane to Amsterdam and one more that will take us to Oslo, Norway. That's the capital of Norway and where the embassy is. We're looking for a guy by the name of Nicko Borge. The only book I have to help me prepare for this trip is a travel guide to Scandinavia Grandma bought me in the airport, and the section on Norway is kind of small, so I'm going to be flying by the seat of my pants, as my dad would have said.

But this is all TOP SECRET!! You can't tell ANYONE!! (You know I don't usually use two exclamation points. Sister Bernadette broke us of that habit in like 5th grade, so you know how important this is.) My mom doesn't even know anything about this, so really, don't tell.

I'm running out of room, but I promise to write

again when I can to give you the low down. Maybe say a prayer to Saint Anthony for me. I know my dad isn't lost, but we need to find out how he died, so it's kind of the same. Close enough, anyway. I'm sure Saint Anthony won't mind.

Your best friend,
Agnes

Dad had lots of cool sayings like *flying by the seat of your pants*, which means to act on instinct [*n: an act or course of action that is automatic rather than learned*] rather than by a set plan or instructions. I know the definition because I took it out of the idiom dictionary in the DeSoto library (the place I live in Wisconsin – the city not the library, though Peggy says I might as well live at the library, I'm there so much). I wrote it down in my composition notebook. You probably have a book just like it in your library too. I wonder where my dad learned all his idioms from.

I fold the letter and slip it in the envelope I brought from home. I had anticipated [*v: to think of something that will or might happen in the future*] using it to write to Peggy when I was in Turkey, but because of all the running around I was doing with

Yusuf, trying to find out what Grandma was hiding, I didn't end up having time. I was given a postcard with a picture of an Air France airplane on the front from the pretty French flight attendant when we got on board. But what I had to write to Peggy needed to be sealed in an envelope. The Air France stewardesses have pill hats on just like the Pan Am ones did, but they have a wreath of gold leaves with a flying horse in the middle embroidered on the front of their hats. The hats and the knee-length dress sets are navy blue instead of Pan Am's sky-blue. They have a lot of makeup on too and smile just as much as the Pan Am stewardesses do. If Peggy decides to become a flight attendant, she wouldn't mind wearing the makeup; she's always trying out her older sister's mascara, lipstick, and blush, but I don't think Peggy can smile as much as these ladies do.

Now Grandma Agee and I are a team, like Charlie Chan and his two kids (I can't remember their names) or Sherlock Holmes and Dr. Watson. I'm really excited that she is going to keep looking for information about my dad and that Grandma wants me to help. So I've got to do what Mr. Morrison, our neighbor, always tells us kids: *Carpe diem*! Seize the day! I did pretty good doing just that when I was in Turkey. Of course, having Yusuf along really helped. If I think about it, I have done a lot of new things.

I had my first plane ride (and got sick).

I got my Grandma Barb's bee pin back all by myself.

I met and made a new friend, someone I would never have predicted would turn out to be my friend.

And I confessed to Grandma what Yusuf and I had been doing: following her to the US Consulate and the Spice Market, and listened in on her conversations. I had no choice, really; I couldn't let Yusuf take the blame.

My mom would be so proud if she knew all the adventures I've had without hardly cracking open a book. And Peggy too. She thinks I should get out more, just like my mom does. She always wants me to go swimming and ice skating and stuff. And I don't mind doing those things; it's just that I like reading more. I've memorized a special Latin phrase that says it all: *Quot libros, quam breve tempus* – So many books, so little time. Peggy always rolls her eyes whenever I say that, but it's true. I even get her to read, now and then, if it's a really good book.

So I'm on my way to Norway. I want to be able to tell my mom and my brothers what happened to my dad. It's sinking in more and more that he's really gone, and I think it would help all of us if we knew the truth. I know it would help me. But if I'm going to help Grandma find out what really happened, I need more information. And the person I need to talk to is sitting right beside me.

I turn to my grandmother. She's reading the book she picked up in the bookstore when she was buying me the travel guide to Scandinavia. It's a really thick book titled *Hawaii* by the author James Michener. I really don't get why adults like to read such big books. It would be interesting to learn about Hawaii, but I think I'd probably die of old age before I finished a book that big. I hope she doesn't get mad at me if I ask her a few questions about my dad. But I figure since the cat is out of the bag now, she shouldn't care. (*The cat is out of the bag* is an idiom Aaron likes to use when he's trying to sound older than he is. He's fourteen – only two years older than me – but he likes to think he's closer to Adam's age – sixteen.) When the cat is out of the bag, it means the truth isn't hidden anymore, and it's not going to be hidden again. If you have a cat, you understand. If you don't have a cat, believe me, you'd get ripped to shreds by the cat's claws if you tried to put one in a bag. It's similar but not quite the same as the idiom *it's like herding cats*. My mom uses that one all the time with Peter, Max, and Danny, my younger brothers. Cats don't like bags or any other form of confinement [*n: the act of keeping a person or animal in a place*], and neither do my younger brothers. They are "free spirits," as Mrs. Anderson – Peggy's mom – would say. I'm not sure what a free spirit is but I think it's adult code for weird.

"Grandma, I was wondering...You said Dad was a spy, but what kind of spying did he do? Who did he spy on?"

"I don't really know, Agnes. Your father only told me he worked for the CIA because I had figured it out and asked him about it. He said no one was supposed to know. Then he agreed it was a good idea if someone knew, in case..." My grandmother stops talking because we both know something did happen, but we just don't know what that "something" was. "...In case somethin' happened te him. He didn't want your mother te find out; he didn't want te worry her none. She has enough te handle with all those boys."

"I can't argue with you on that one," I say. My brothers get into all kinds of trouble. Me? Well, trouble just seems to find me all on its own.

"And you told Uncle Bob?"

Grandma closes her eyes and shakes her head as if she just got a whiff of a moldy cheese. "Yes, I made the mistake of tellin' your Uncle Bob."

I have to smile as I think about how Uncle Bob got a talking to from Grandma at Dad's funeral when he almost spilled the beans about my dad working for the CIA as a spy.

"Did Dad's partner in Turkey, Mr. Bahar, say anything about their last mission?"

"I'm afraid not, only that it was top secret. I'm guessin' that's why they told us he had his car accident in Turkey, even though the letter I got from your father just days before he died was postmarked from Norway."

I had forgotten how Grandma figured out something was suspicious about my dad's death. She must be a pretty smart cookie to have noticed the postmark on that letter. I'm not sure how a cookie is smart but that's what people say and that's what my grandma is, smart – not a cookie. I'm glad I've got her on my side.

I purse my lips, unsure how she's going to take my next question. "You don't happen to have that letter with you, do you? There might be some clue in it that you didn't notice when you first read it."

Grandma tips her head and looks pleased with my idea. She picks up her purse from under her legs and begins to dig through it.

She finally pulls out a small envelope and holds

it out to me. I'm almost afraid to take it. It's a harmless, white envelope, but the moment I see my dad's scribbled handwriting on the front, my heart starts to race and I get really warm. It's the last thing my dad ever wrote, and for some reason, I'm kind of afraid to read it.

Grandma Agee notices my reaction and moves the letter back to her lap. "I can read it to ya if ya like," she says as she opens up the envelope and pulls out the small piece of paper.

I reach out for it. "No. No, I can do it. It's just that..."

"No need to explain, Agnes."

And just as I reach for the letter, it suddenly disappears.

Chapter Two

Remember when I said trouble just seems to find me? Well, here's a perfect example. One minute I have my dad's last-ever letter in my hand and the next minute I don't. It's not that it went up in smoke or disappeared into thin air; it was something entirely different, and it wasn't my fault, I swear it!

Both Grandma and I are leaning over our seats, looking at the man who is now face down on the floor in the aisle of the airplane. Somehow the man knocked the letter out of my hand as he fell.

"Oh, I'm so sorry," he says as he picks himself up off the floor. "I don't know what I tripped on...." he says, then looks at the floor behind him, but there is nothing there.

"Are you all right?" Grandma asks.

The man has blond hair that is cut very short on the sides and is perfectly flat on the top, so flat you could set a cup of coffee on top of his head and you wouldn't spill a drop. I wonder how he gets all the hairs to stick straight up like that. My gym teacher at St. James, Mr. Keefer, has a haircut just like that.

The man pulls down on his suit jacket and straightens his tie. I notice that he has the oddest-looking tiepin I've ever seen. My dad's tiepins are just a straight piece of metal the color of gold or silver (I'm sure they're not real gold or silver. I think it would cost a lot to make a gold or silver tiepin, and we don't own anything that expensive). This man's tiepin has a shiny, dark thing that looks like a stone the size of a quarter attached to it.

"Yes. Yes, I'm just fine. My fault. Entirely my fault," he says in a deep voice.

Grandma looks down at my dad's letter that is now lying slightly crumbled on the floor of the plane.

"Oh dear, your letter." The man reaches down and picks it up. He attempts to straighten it out, then holds it in front of him with one hand, examining his handiwork, while he adjusts his tie with the other. "Good as new," he says with a smile and hands the letter to my grandmother. Then just like that, he's gone.

Grandma Agee and I look at each other and we both shrug our shoulders.

I sit on the edge of my seat and peer over just the tops of the plane seats behind me. I don't want the man seeing me, but he is nowhere in sight. He must have sat back down.

Grandma Agee hands me the letter, and I sit back in my seat, take a deep breath, and begin to read.

Dear Mum,

I hope this letter finds you well. I'm sorry I haven't written in a while but I've been busy with extra safety training for my new assignment. I have a bit of time while I'm waiting to catch a plane, so I finally have a few minutes to myself to write to you. I am meeting up with a group that is helping us with our current assignment. I can't tell you who they are or where I am going, of course, but it's the culmination of a lot of years of work, which has gotten me out from behind my desk and back to doing something I really enjoy, so I'm happy about that.

I put the letter down for a minute and think about the things I know my dad enjoyed doing. (I'm getting better with the past tense thing, but it doesn't make me feel any better about him being gone.) He liked to hunt and fish, but I don't imagine spies have any reason to hunt or fish. He liked to read, like Uncle Bob said, but probably the only thing someone working in the CIA would be reading is a report of some sort. Most of the rest of the time when my dad was home, he worked on the house, helped Max with his airplane and car models, or was at Uncle Roger's farm with my brother Peter. I would guess it's highly unlikely that the CIA has a farm, so that can't be it either. I go back to reading the letter.

> *The downside to this new assignment is that I've been away from Mary and the kids more. There is also the possibility that I will be put in harm's way, but since the assignment is critical to the safety of our country and many others at this juncture in time, it's a risk I am willing to take. I know you and Mary would agree with me if you knew the whole story.*
>
> *Keep me in your prayers.*
>
> *Love,*
>
> *Patrick*

I pull out my pocket dictionary, the one my mother got me for this trip, and I look up "juncture" [*n: an important point in a process or activity*]. I open my composition notebook and put the word and its definition on my "Cool Words" list. I'll have to use that word again. It will make me sound smart, for sure! I've already copied common Norwegian phrases in my notebook that should come in handy: *Hallo* (*hah-lõõ* [oo like in soon] – Hello); *Snakker du engelsk?* (**snah**kerr dew **ehn**gerlsk – Do you speak English?); *Jeg forstår ikke* (yæ [æ like in at] *foshtewr ikker* – I don't understand); and, of course, *Hvor er badet* (*voor air **baa**der* – Where is the bathroom?). The usual ones. I also looked up "thank you" – *Takk* (*tahk*) since that was one I needed in Istanbul but didn't write down before I left. I had to ask Vasil, the Zanzibar Hotel manager, how to say that in Turkish. And just so you know, æ isn't a typing mistake; that's one of the extra vowel sounds they have in Norway.

"Do you think we'll be able to buy an American paper in the airport in Paris?" I ask.

"I have no idea. I've never been to Paris before, let alone in their airport. Why do you need an American paper?"

"Well, Dad says the assignment he was on..." I pick up my dad's letter to make sure I get his exact words correct, "was 'critical to the safety of our country,' so I thought maybe if we watched the papers for a while, we might be able to figure out what his assignment was related to."

Grandma gives me a half smile. "You're smart as a whip, aren't ya, girl?"

I'm guessing that smart as a whip is an idiom because how can a whip be smart? But I know it's a compliment by the smile on my grandma's face and the way she says it, so I can't help but blush.

I try to think about what I heard on the news before we left for our trip. I remember there was a big article in the paper about the Freedom Riders: some young people who rode buses from towns in the North to towns in the South. The article talked about people who followed one of the buses and threw a bomb on the bus. And when the young people tried to get off the burning bus, they beat them up, even the women. I didn't believe it at first, but when I asked Mom about it, she was so upset she wouldn't discuss it. And the only thing Dad said was that it was shameful. I asked Adam what the deal was, and he said they bombed the bus because both white and black people were on the bus together and the people that followed them didn't like that. I know from articles in the newspaper and watching the news on TV that there are some white people who don't like black people, but that doesn't explain why they couldn't ride the bus together. I just don't get it, but then I don't get a lot of things that seem to bother adults. And I can't see how the CIA would care about what happened to the Freedom Riders. To me that seems like a matter for the police.

In April there was a lot of talk about how the Soviets sent a man into orbit around the earth. I'm not sure why all the news people were so excited because I don't think he was up there much more than an hour. After that happened, JFK (that's short for John Fitzgerald Kennedy – our president, of course) asked Congress for money to not only send a man into orbit but to actually land a man on the moon. Can you imagine?! I saw it on a news clip in the theater when Peggy and I brought our younger siblings to see *101 Dalmatians*. I think the president did that because in early May, when one of our astronauts tried to orbit the earth like the Soviet one did, he didn't get up far enough. I don't really get why everyone wants to get to the moon so badly. I asked my science teacher, Mr. Pearson, what was on the moon that was so all-fired special. He said probably nothing much, but no one has done it before, and it would be a major scientific feat if we could be the first to land on the moon. I agree, it would be pretty cool but pretty scary for the man on the top of that rocket!

A

Soon after lunch, we prepare to land in Le Bourget Airport in France. I remembered what happened the last time I flew on a full stomach, so I only eat a roll and the two small sugar cookies on my lunch tray. My stomach still does its usual back flip as we circle the airport for our landing, but at least I don't toss my cookies (as Max would say). Those cookies wouldn't look so good coming back up.

The landing is smooth and soon we're taxiing to our gate. We come to a stop, and like before, everyone around us, except Grandma and me, gets up and pulls their things from the overhead bins. Grandma hands me my gloves and starts to put on her own.

"Attencion, attencion, *Mesdames et Messieurs,*" a man says in French. I would guess it's the pilot.

Most everyone stops talking and moving to listen. The man makes an announcement in French, and when he's done, the people who understand French groan, so I know it's not good news. Then the man goes on to repeat what he said, in English this time.

"Vee are most sorry to inform you zat vee are unable to disembark at zis time."

Now all the people that understand English groan.

"Zere eez an incident at ze airport and vee have been asked to remain inside our plane. Your flight attendants wiell be most happy to serve you a cocktail vhile you are vaiting. Vee appreciate your patience and zank you again for flying Air Fraunce."

A man standing just behind us leans over our seats and says in a slurred voice, "We better get a drink. Paid enough for this flight I could'a bought a car and drove here!"

"Then why didn't ya," I hear my grandmother mutter under her breath.

Two flight attendants immediately rush toward the man, smiles pasted on their faces. They get him to sit back down and put a drink in his hand before he has a chance to say anything more. From the trouble he is having talking, I think he has had enough to drink already, but adults don't listen to kids, so they probably don't care what I think.

It is an hour before they let us out of the plane. Now I have not just one new set of airline wings but five, one for each of my brothers. (I know Adam won't want his, so I'll give that one to Peggy.) I also have four extra bags of peanuts and three extra cookies wrapped in my handkerchief. That was in addition to the three bags of nuts and two cookies I have already eaten. I also have a brand new deck of Air France playing cards. They are blue and white and really slippery, unlike the worn-out cards we have at home. While we waited, I taught Grandma how to play Go Fish and War, and she taught me an Irish card game called Snap. Grandma had another cocktail, like most of the adults, and I had another Coke, so I am pretty full when we go down the stairs to exit the plane.

We see police lights leaving the airport as we walk to the terminal, but we don't find out what all the fuss was about until we get inside. Apparently, a ballet dancer by the name of Rudolf Nureyev defected to France. I don't know what it means to defect so I ask Grandma Agee. She says that if you defect, you don't want to live in your home country anymore. She says that it's not very nice in Russia since the "Big War," and "They're leavin' East Germany like fleas off a drownin' cat." Grandma explains that the Russians got control of the eastern part of Germany after WWII and some of the Germans that live there don't want to stay.

"Maybe Russia should spend more money on the people that live there than on spaceships that send men up in space," I say.

Grandma nods her head in agreement. "No truer words were ever said."

A

The plane rides to Amsterdam and Norway go pretty well, considering we're on a much smaller plane on both trips – a prop job like the one Peggy and I saw in the Humphrey Bogart movie, *Casablanca*. These planes might be a bit bigger than the one in the movie but not by much. There are two seats on one side of the plane and only one seat on the other – thirty in all – and the bins over our heads don't have doors on them, so when we bounce around a bit as we land in the Oslo airport in Norway, Grandma's purse falls down on her head. There isn't much room in front of the seat, so Grandma had to put her purse and my bag above her head.

"Jesus, Mary, and Joseph!" Grandma yells out when her purse comes tumbling down, waking us both out of a sound sleep.

We both had been sleeping because we flew into Amsterdam really late and had to spend the night in the airport. Our flight to Fornebu Airport in Oslo – the capital of Norway – was scheduled at six in the morning, and Grandma didn't want to spend the money on a room for just a few hours. I can see her point, but let me tell you, it's really hard to sleep in an airport chair. At least I was able to rest my head on Grandma's lap. Grandma had to try sleeping sitting up. I don't think it worked very well. Luckily, my bag is heavy enough that it stays in place.

I get out of my seat and help the stewardess and Grandma pick all of Grandma's things off the floor.

I find the picture of the boy that Grandma was looking at on our way to Istanbul, the boy that looks like Adam. I finally realize it's not Adam because this young boy has on a cap and is wearing knickers.

I hand the picture back to Grandma. "Is that my dad?"

Grandma's scowl instantly softens, and she takes the picture from me so gently it seems like she's afraid it will fall apart in her hand.

"That's my Patrick," Grandma says.

"I'm sorry but you'll have to get back in your seat and buckle in. We're about to land," the stewardess says.

When I stand up to crawl back over Grandma Agee, I look to the back of the plane and I see the strangest thing. The man with the flattop haircut from the Air France flight is sitting in the back of the plane, and he's looking right at me.

Chapter Three

There is a place at the airport where we are able to exchange our American dollars and stray Turkish lira for kroners (the money they have in Norway), and the nice lady at the exchange place also gives us a map of the city when Grandma asks her the location of the American Embassy. Grandma thinks the embassy is the best place to start to look for Mr. Borge. "If they don't know Mr. Borge, they should know where the Norwegian Intelligence Agency is." The lady also tells us we can take a bus from the airport to the city center, and from there we can take a tram that will take us right past the embassy, which also is in downtown Oslo. Good thing her English is pretty good because neither Grandma nor

I know Norwegian. I'm guessing she must get a lot of people visiting Norway that speak English for her to practice on because her English is very good.

We get off the bus by city hall and walk one block to what is obviously the main street in Oslo, Karl Johans Gate (*Kall Yo-hans Gaa-te* – gate is what they say for street in Norwegian). There is a park on one side of the street that's about three blocks long. On the other side are expensive looking shops and restaurants. Like in Istanbul, lots of restaurants have tables outside on the sidewalk, and since the sun is warm and bright, Grandma wants to eat outside. We pick a place called The Grand Café because it's busy. Grandma says that's a sure way to tell if the food is any good. It's kind of fun to sit outside and eat, like you're on a picnic, but you don't have to sit on the ground and get ants and dirt in your food. I think if they tried this in downtown De Soto, you might get eaten by mosquitoes. Actually, Grandma is eating lunch; I'm eating breakfast. Once we got in the air on that small plane to Amsterdam, I decided it was best for me – and the rest of the passengers – if I didn't eat anything, not even a piece of bread. I didn't eat anything on the plane ride to Oslo either, so now I'm famished! [*adj: very hungry* – but you probably could have figured that out.]

Luckily, they seem to have chickens and pigs

everywhere, so I order eggs, ham, and toast with some really good orange jam Grandma says is marmalade. I've never had marmalade before, and it's kind of bitter and sweet at the same time. In between bites of food, I ask Grandma a question that has been bothering me all morning.

"Grandma, did you see that blond-haired guy on the plane?"

"The man who fell on your father's letter? Of course I did, Agnes, I spoke with him."

"No, I mean did you notice he was on the same plane to Oslo that we were on?"

Grandma looks at me as if I'd said I'd seen a ghost. "Are you sure it was the same man?"

"I'm positive. When we were walking to the terminal, I watched him leave the plane. He had on a hat and different suit and tie but he had that same ugly tiepin."

I lean in close and lower my voice. "Do you think he's following us?"

"Now you're talkin' jibberish, child. If it was the same man, and I'm not sayin' it was, mind ya, it's just a coincidence. Oslo's a very busy place. Maybe the man has work here."

In case you don't know what coincidence means, it's when two things happen at the same time by accident but they seem to have some connection. I can tell I'm not going to convince Grandma that it was the same man, even though I know it was, so I go back to finishing my ham and eggs. But I'm going to keep my eyes peeled for him, just in case. Keeping your eyes peeled doesn't mean I am going to do anything disgusting to my eyes; it just means I'm going to watch out for him, in case we just happen to cross paths again. Maybe Grandma's right, but then again, maybe not. If he is following us, there has to be a reason.

A

After we eat, we head for the embassy but decide to walk up Karls Johans Gate instead of taking the tram, so we can make a small detour to the Royal Palace. My travel guide says it's the residence of the Norwegian Royal Family. I know England has a King and Queen, but I didn't know Norway did too. You can't miss the palace; it sits on a rise at the top of the street, so anywhere you go on Karl Johans Gate, you see it. It's a really big, rectangular building that is made of light-colored brick – gray brick on the first floor and tan on the second and third floors. It has a set of columns in the middle that run from the second to the third floor in an area that sticks out from the building and looks like a really tall front porch. There is a large lawn all around the building with lots of flowers and well-manicured trees [manicured is an adjective: *to make (something, such as a lawn or a garden) look neat, smooth, and attractive.* It works for fingernails too. That's how I learned that word. Peggy's older sister wants to go to beauty school so she gave Peggy and me a manicure and pedicure, which is the same thing as a manicure but for your feet.] I want to take a tour, but when I hint at the idea, Grandma says we have "bigger fish to fry," whatever that means, and she turns and heads back down to the street. I'm starting to get an idea of where my dad got all his idioms from.

It probably is a good idea to pass on the palace tour since Grandma would have a hard time lugging her suitcase around on a tour, and I'd probably get tired too. We take a side path on the palace grounds toward Henrik Ibsens (*Hine-rrick Ib-sens*) Gate, walk a few more blocks, and before you know it, we're in front of the US Embassy.

After seeing the palace, this building looks really boring. It's black and has small, narrow windows all along each of its four floors. There is a very official looking man in a cap and uniform standing outside the front door. When we walk up the front steps, he holds the door open for us but he doesn't say a word.

We walk up to the receptionist at a tall desk in the lobby and set our suitcases down.

"May I help you?" the lady says with a smile. She speaks English very well, but she has got a bit of an accent, so I'm guessing she's Norwegian.

"Yes. We're looking for Mr. Nicko Borge. He works for the Norwegian Intelligence Agency, specifically EI 4," my grandmother says like she's asking for directions to the bathroom.

The lady frowns, looks at me, then looks back to my grandmother as if she's not sure she heard the question correctly.

"Do you understand English?" Grandma asks.

"Yes. Yes, of course I do. It's just that we don't usually get people, particularly women, asking for the Etterretningstjenesten, the Intelligence Service. Is there a problem?"

Wow, that's a mouth full!

Grandma looks at me as if I might be able to answer the lady's question, then luckily, she turns back to the receptionist. "Yes, there is a problem, and it's important that I talk with Mr. Borge in EI 4. My son worked for the CIA, and he was in Norway recently where he died under suspicious circumstances."

My head whips up to stare at my grandmother.

I can't believe what she just said. She didn't tell my mother the truth about my father's death but she's willing to tell a complete stranger in a strange country. I give up trying to understand adults.

"I might have some information about my son that Mr. Borge would like to know."

"Do you mean Nikolai Borge of E14?" the woman says almost in a whisper, like it isn't something you should say out loud.

My grandmother hesitates before answering. "I suppose."

"Um...Let me see if I can find him." The woman picks up her phone, then looks back to Grandma Agee. "May I say who is asking for Mr. Borge?" (The lady says Mr. Borge's name different than Grandma and I have been saying it. She pronounces it Boor-gea [gea as in ge-t])

"Mrs. Agnes Kelly. My son is Patrick Daniel Kelly."

The woman dials the phone and after a few seconds starts to rattle off something in Norwegian that neither Grandma nor I can understand, that is until she says Grandma's name and then my dad's. I would guess she is speaking Norwegian in case we're spies or something.

I lean close to Grandma and whisper, "What is it that Mr. Borge would like to know about dad?"

"I don't know," Grandma whispers back and

gives me a wink. "I said I might have some information Mr. Borge would like to know, I didn't say I did."

My eyes go wide in surprise. *Tricky, Grandma, very tricky!*

The receptionist eventually puts the phone down. "I'm sorry but Mr. Borge is working in Bodø at the moment."

(If you're wondering what that funny ø in Bodø is, it's one of those extra vowels I mentioned earlier. It sounds like "ir" in the word fir, like the tree. I noticed the different spelling when I found the city on the map of Norway in my travel guide to Scandinavia. Just so you know.)

"Bodø?" Grandma and I say in unison [*n: at the same time*].

"It's a city in north-central Norway, quite a ways from here," she replies. "I'm sorry."

My Grandma lets out a big sigh and says thank you. She picks up her suitcase and turns to leave. She motions with her head for me to do the same. I didn't see him before but there is another man in uniform standing by the inside door, and he opens it to let us out. Before I go out the door, I glance back at the receptionist. She's on the phone again and staring directly at me as she's talking. I can tell she's talking about us because she immediately looks away and gets all red in the face the minute I catch her staring.

A

I walk up to Grandma, who's standing on the sidewalk, digging in her purse. She pulls out the Oslo city map and unfolds it.

"I'm sorry, Grandma. We came a long way for nothing."

Grandma studies the map like she didn't hear what I had said. After a minute she folds it up again, picks up her suitcase, and starts walking back toward Karl Johans Gate. "Come along, Agnes," she says over her shoulder.

I run to catch up.

"We *have* come a long way." Grandma has a very determined look on her face. "But it isn't for nothing. We've found out where Mr. Borge is, didn't we. She looks down at me and gives me another wink. Grandma digs farther into her purse and pulls out Dad's letter and looks at the front, then hands it to me. "Look at the postmark."

It's a bit smudged but I finally make out *Bodø, Norway.*

"And we're going to go to Bodø to find him," Grandma says.

Chapter Four

I look in my Scandinavian travel guide to show Grandma where Bodø is. Norway is a really long, skinny country that sits mostly north-south, right next to Sweden. According to my travel guide, the top three quarters of it is only seven or eight kilometers wide. As the lady at the embassy said, Bodø is in the north-central part of Norway. In fact, it's so far north, it's above the Arctic Circle. Half of Alaska is above the Arctic Circle too, so that gives you an idea that it's pretty far up there. Because Bodø is so far from Oslo, Grandma wants to take the train to Bodø instead of another plane. She said plane fares are pretty expensive, and she wants to save some money, even though it will take us longer to get there. The train station is about twenty blocks away, at the opposite end of Karl Johans Gate, so we hop on the tram. It lets us off right in front of the station.

I've never been on a tram before so it's kind of fun. A tram is like a bus that runs on rails right down the middle of the street and is powered by electricity instead of gas. I know this because there is a metal pole that sticks up from the top of the tram that touches a really thick wire that is suspended [*v: to hang so as to be free on all sides except at the point of support*] above the street. When the tram's metal pole loses contact with the wire, it sends off an arc of electricity and makes a crackling sound. It's just like when my brother Max rubs his feet on the carpet and touches my arm. That's just static electricity, so it's not as powerful as the electricity that runs these trams, but it still gives me a good shock. That's why Max does it, of course.

The train station is cool looking, built kind of boxy, like the royal palace, but the brick on the train station is yellow and it's only two stories high. Inside there is a big open area that goes all the way to the ceiling with skylights at the top.

Lots of English-speaking people must take trains too because the person we get our tickets from speaks English very well, just like the person at the airport.

We have about an hour to kill before our train leaves, so Grandma lets me do a little souvenir shopping in a small store inside the station while she sits on a bench to rest. I like how Grandma Agee trusts me and lets me go shopping on my own, even though we're in a strange town in a foreign country. Grandma doesn't want to venture [*v: to face the risk and danger*] from the station; she doesn't want to miss our train. (Just in case you're wondering, Grandma taught me the word "venture," and I kind of like it so I thought I'd use it too. It's almost like the word "adventure" and we are sure on one of those!)

Grandma told me Norway is known for its trolls, so I buy a small troll for Peggy and one for me. Trolls are really ugly with big feet, a big head, and a big nose. They even have trolls with only one eye, but even *I* think those trolls look kind of creepy, so I stick with the two-eyed ones. I buy Peggy a girl troll, but she will still think the troll is really gross, so it will be fun to see the look on her face when I give it to her. I already picked up souvenirs for everyone in my family in Istanbul because I thought I was going home from there, but I wanted to pick up something extra for Peggy since she's my best friend, really, my only close friend. Mom says if I didn't have my nose stuck in a book so much, I'd have more friends. But I don't need more friends; Peggy does the job just fine. I still might try and find something else for my mother too, since I'm thinking she's not going to be so excited about Grandma taking me on something she would probably call "a wild goose chase." That's one of those idioms I'm sure you've heard your parents say when someone asks them for something that they think they will never find. I've never tried to chase a goose. Aaron said they can be really mean, so when we see them near the Mississippi, I pretty much leave them alone. They are big birds too, and I wouldn't want one of them chasing after me.

Remember when I told you things seem to happen to me that are no fault of my own, like when my bee pin fell out of my hair from the hotel balcony right into a lady's cream pie? Well, the same thing happens at the train station. As I'm walking back toward my grandmother, I notice my saddle shoe has come untied, so I bend down to tie it. I set the trolls beside me so they can see how it's done. The trolls are barefoot, probably because they have really big feet and they can't find shoes that fit, but shoe tying is a good skill to learn, even for a troll.

Just as I'm tucking one rabbit ear under another,

Peggy's troll decides she can't wait for me. She takes a trip of her own when a lady kicks Peggy's troll and sends it flying. The lady has got a bunch of bags in her hands, and she's talking in what sounds like French to another lady carrying just as many bags. She's so busy with her conversation that she's oblivious [*adj: without active conscious knowledge or awareness*] to what just happened. (I love the word oblivious, don't you? It sounds so sophisticated [*adj: highly complicated or developed*]. I use it all the time when I'm describing my brothers.) I don't think trolls are meant to fly, real ones or pretend ones, and as I watch Peggy's troll arch smoothly and soundlessly through the air, I'm sure she's going to drop onto the hard tile floor of the station and break into a million pieces. Kind of like Humpty Dumpty, where all the King's horses and all the King's men couldn't put him back together again.

But I'm happy to report that that's not what happens! You're not going to believe this, but Miss Troll hits a lady's backside and drops right down into the bag of a man standing right behind her. The lady turns around and scowls at the man, who is facing away from her and doesn't have a clue what just happened. The lady picks up her things and moves away from him in a huff. I try not to laugh as I hurry up and finish tying my shoe. I pick up my troll (a boy troll) and run after Peggy's. The man who owns the bag Miss Troll fell into is looking up at the arrival and departure sign on the wall above everyone's heads and doesn't even notice what is going on. I sneak up behind him and just as I reach inside his bag and grab hold of the little flying beast, the man looks down.

I'm about to apologize and try and explain what just happened when I am frozen in place. It's not because I've done something wrong – it is my troll, after all – but I'm frozen because of what I see. It's the same man, the man with the blond hair from the airport! I'm not sure it's him at first because now his hair is cut real short all over his head, like my dad does to my brothers at the beginning of the summer, and for some reason he has changed his suit since getting off the plane this morning. He was wearing a dark blue suit when he got off the plane, but now he has on a light gray one. I'm finally convinced it's him when he quickly bends down to pick up his bag and that big, ugly tiepin dangles right in front of me. He notices me staring at it, and he buttons his suit jacket shut and rushes into the crowd without saying a word or looking back.

A

"Grandma, Grandma! You're not going to believe this!" I say, out of breath.

After the man with funny tiepin left, I ran after him but couldn't find him. I looked all over the station, but he seemed to have vanished into thin air.

"You know that man that tripped on the Air France plane and fell on Dad's letter, the man I saw on our plane to Oslo? I just saw him! I just saw him again!" I say as fast as I can talk.

"Slow down, child. Slow down and tell me again, but this time so I can understand ya."

So I tell her all about my shoe and the flying troll hitting the lady in the backside and about whose bag the troll landed in. Then when I get to the part about his hair and clothes being different, she gives me a skeptical [*adj: marked by skepticism, n: an attitude of doubt in general or toward a particular object*] look.

"That sounds like a yarn," Grandma says.

"A yarn?" I say. I'm picturing a ball of my Grandma Barb's brightly-colored yarn that she used to make afghans and baby blankets, but that doesn't make sense.

"A tale...sounds like you're tellin' me a tale."

"Oh, no, I'm positive it was him. I got a real good

look at his cold-looking blue eyes, and he still had on that ugly tiepin."

Grandma looks at me as if I've got a screw loose. That's an idiom Aaron uses. I would guess having a "screw loose" is like a machine that has a part that isn't screwed down tight so it isn't working quite right, except it refers to a person's mind and not a machine.

"Even if he changed suits, there'd be no cause for the man to cut his hair."

"Unless he didn't want us to recognize him."

"Why would he care if we recognized him?" she says in a softer voice, almost like she's asking herself the question instead of me.

"Maybe that lady at the embassy told him we had visited, and he took a chance that we'd be here at the train station. You didn't notice, but she called someone as we were leaving. I caught her talking on the phone, and she was looking right at me. She had the same guilty look on her face that my brothers do when my mom catches them with a hand in the cookie jar."

"That might be a bit of a stretch, Agnes. But now that you mention it, I think the man on the plane did have steely-blue eyes."

I smile. Maybe Grandma is finally starting to believe me.

"If it *were* the same man, it would be more than a bit suspicious for him te all of a sudden feel the need te get a new haircut."

"Yeah, like dad's death was suspicious," I remind her.

Grandma looks at me and nods her head in agreement, then she looks over my head at the people milling about as if she can spot the man from where we're sitting.

"I looked all around for him after he grabbed his bag and ducked into the crowd, but I couldn't find him anywhere," I explain.

A man on the intercom announces something in what is probably Norwegian, then French, and finally in English. "First call for the 4:10 to Trondheim. First call."

"That's us," Grandma says and stands. She picks up her purse and her suitcase. I do the same, and she directs me to train platform number four. "Well, if he is really following us, Agnes, and we see him on the train, we've got a much better chance of catchin' 'im and findin' out what he's up to."

A

On the platform the train cars stretch out farther than I can even see to count. Grandma shows our tickets to a man in a dark blue uniform. He wears a hat similar to a policeman's hat, and he directs us to the correct car. A man dressed in a similar uniform standing just outside our train car takes our cases and helps Grandma Agee up the first tall step.

The train car we get into has two rows of bench seats on both sides of a narrow aisle. We pick an empty seat, and, of course, Grandma lets me sit by the window.

I've never been on a train before so I'm pretty excited. I've seen lots of trains, of course. There is a set of train tracks right along the Mississippi, right next to DeSoto, and there are always trains going up and down along the river. Those trains are mostly coal cars, black oil tankers, cars hauling cut tree trunks, or boxy freight cars. We have passenger trains that go by sometimes too but not as often. The coolest passenger train is the Zephyr. That's a sleek [*adj: smooth and glossy as if polished*], all-silver train that looks like it's right out of one of Aaron's Flash Gordon or Buck Rogers comics. Our train car is pretty plain looking, other than the bright-red, cloth bench seats. The seats face each other and have a large headrest that is covered in a white cloth that can be taken off and cleaned. There is a small table between the seats that is attached to the wall and can be flipped up in place.

It takes us a bit of time to get outside of the city, but before you know it, instead of seeing the backsides of buildings, we're seeing trees and hills. After about a half hour, we pull up next to a small river that gets a bit bigger with each passing mile.

I tug on Grandma Agee's sleeve.

"Look Grandma, we're following a river."

"That's the Andelva," the man across from us says. "It will take us to the Vorma River, which is even wider, then to Mjøsa (*mew-sa*) Lake, Norway's largest lake."

The man has a thick Norwegian accent.

I pull my Scandinavian travel guide out of my bag and open to the Norwegian map. It's too small to see anything but a blue line and small blob where the Lake Mjøsa opens at its widest point.

The man leans over and looks at my small map. "Here..." he says, then pulls a paper map out of his bag. He flips up the small table, opens up his map, and turns it so I can see. It's a full size map of Norway. He finds the fattest part of the lake and moves his finger down about half way to Oslo. "We are about here."

I smile and nod.

He reaches out his hand to me. "My name is Georg."

I suspect that is George in American English but he says it like Gay-org. Georg has curly blond hair cut short to his head like a helmet. He has soft blue eyes, a pleasant smile, and a sturdy [*adj: firm*] handshake. I can't help but smile back.

"I'm Agnes Kelly and this is my grandmother. She's Agnes Kelly too, so everyone calls her Grandma Agee. Well, everyone in my family, that is."

Georg reaches out to shake my grandma's hand.

"Please to meet you, Mrs. Kelly. This is my wife, Inger."

Inger shakes our hands. "Nice meeting you," she says in a quiet voice, like she's not quite sure of her words.

My attention is diverted [*v: to take (attention) away from someone or something*] out the window again as the sound of the metal wheels of the train car change when we cross what must be a bridge. I can see a large body of water below, and when I look across the train car and out the window on the other side, I can see more water. That must be Mjøsa Lake, which according to the map, is very long and skinny. I look back down at the map to confirm my theory.

I don't know about you, but I love maps. My mom says I shouldn't say I LOVE an inanimate [*adj: not living or capable of life*] object like a map, but I figure it's better than saying I really, really, really like maps. I think it's partly because my dad likes...I mean liked maps too. He had this humongous atlas of the world, and we'd spend hours looking at the different places in Europe he went in the war or places he traveled on his trips for work. Now that I know he was a spy, it makes more sense why he'd travel all over the place. I often wondered why he'd have to go to England or Pakistan or Turkey to sell insurance. But he said there were government employees all over the world, and I suppose there are. I don't know why I never thought that he could have just sent them information in the mail versus traveling to those countries to talk to them in person.

We make our first stop in a city called Hamar, then about forty-five minutes later we stop in the slightly larger city of Lillehammer (*Lil-a-hammer*). On our way to Lillehammer, we start to see some bigger hills, and the water gets pretty wide. Georg says it's not a river but the top of Mjøsa Lake. It doesn't look any wider than the Mississippi River does outside of DeSoto, though it's not the same brown color. (They don't call it the muddy Mississippi for nothing.)

The map Georg is letting me look at is not just a plain map, it's a topographical map, which means it shows the different elevations of the land. I can tell by looking out my window that the farther west we go, the higher the hills get, but now by looking on the map, I know just how high they are. As we get closer to Dombås (*Dome-baas*), which Georg says is our next stop, there are mountains all around us. (Did you notice another funny vowel – å. That's the third new vowel, if you're keeping track.) The biggest mountain around Dombås is to the south, the left when I look out the window. It's called Skjervkroken (I'm not even going to try to figure out how that is pronounced!) and is 1768 meters high (or 2519 feet). Grandma says there is about three and a quarter feet in a meter, so if you multiply 3.25 X 1768 you get 2519. I'm kind of disappointed that I can't see the top of it today because it's covered in fog or clouds or something. My travel guide tells me Galdhøpiggen is the tallest mountain in the whole country at 2469 meters. (I'll let you figure that out in feet.) I suppose countries name their mountains so that mountain climbers can say "I just climbed Mount Galdhøpiggen," and everyone will be impressed when they look on a topographical map and see how high the mountain really is. I can tell on the really tall mountains that the trees all stop growing at the same point around the mountain top. I pull out my composition notebook and make a note to myself to go to the library when I get back home and find out why trees don't grow above a certain point.

A

We are in the dining car waiting for our dinner of lamb, potatoes, and green beans when I am reminded why we are on this trip. My stomach growls when it gets a whiff of the cooked-meat smell coming from the kitchen. We are sitting with Inger and Georg. Grandma wants to thank the nice Norwegian couple for being so kind to me, answering all of my questions; Georg even gave me his map, so she offered to buy their dinner. I'm about to take a bite of my *leftse (left-sa)* when it falls out of my hands and onto my plate. (Leftse is a really thin potato pancake. You put butter and brown sugar on top of it, then you roll it up to eat. Inger suggested Grandma and I try it while we're waiting for our meal because it's a traditional Norwegian food she thought we would like.) My mouth is stuck open like my jaw is rusted in place. My grandmother looks at me, then over her shoulder at what I'm looking at, and she's frozen in place too. There, at the end of the dining car, is the man with the steel-blue eyes and the ugly tiepin looking right at us.

Then before I have a chance to stand and run up to him to ask him why he's following us, the lights suddenly go out.

Chapter Five

It's only a couple seconds and we can see again, but it's almost like a magic trick: the man has completely disappeared. I don't even think about it; I jump up and run in the only direction he could have gone.

"Agnes!" I hear my grandma say as I dodge under a waiter holding a glass pitcher of water. I look back briefly and see him twirl in place so as not to spill any water on anyone, then I push open the door to the dining car and rush out.

It's windy between the train cars, and the noise of the wheels on the tracks and the air rushing by seem really loud after the quiet dining car, but I can't stop. I've got to find the man who's following us.

I step into the next car, but he's nowhere to be seen, so I pick up speed. I'm halfway through the car and a lady drops her purse into the aisle right in front of me. She leans over to pick it up, but I'm moving too fast to stop. I do the only thing I can do; I leap right over top of her, skirt and all! (She was looking down, so I don't think she saw anything.) I hear her shriek, but I'm not about to slow down. This might be my only chance to find out why the man is following us and what it has to do with my father. I don't see him in the next car either, so I decide maybe I should slow down a bit and look carefully in each seat, in case he's hunched down. We're on a moving train, after all. Where can he go? This car has a bathroom in it, so when I don't find him in any of the seats, I knock on the bathroom door and keep knocking until it opens.

It takes a while but eventually a little kid opens the door. He looks at me like I've lost my marbles. (That's probably an idiom you've heard before. It's similar to having a screw loose.) I search through three more cars before I stumble forward, about to fall flat on my face as the train comes to a complete stop.

I don't hit the floor, though, because a young man reaches out to catch me. "You all right?" he says in English – British English because he's got a British accent. He's sitting with three other guys that look to be a few years older than Adam, who is sixteen. They all have backpacks on their laps like they are just about to leave the train.

"Yes, I'm fine. Thanks," I say and look out the train window to see that we've stopped at the Dombås train station.

I exit the train car, but I stay standing between the cars so I can look out across the platform. It's full of people, some waiting to get on the train and others that have just gotten off. I don't see the man anywhere.

As I make my way back to the dining car, I meet Grandma Agee walking toward me a bit out of breath.

"Lordy, girl. I can't keep runnin' after ya like that. I'm no spring chicken anymore," she says and shakes her head.

Of course, being a chicken in the spring doesn't have anything to do with my grandmother. It's an idiom that means she's not young anymore. Don't ask me how they came up with that one; I have no idea!

"Did you find him?" she asks.

I stop and stare at her. I was expecting her to say something like "What were you thinking running off like that?" or "What if you caught up with that man? After what happened to your father, we don't know what he's capable of," which is what my parents would have said. Well, at least what my mom would have said, since my dad can't say anything to me anymore.

"No. We came into the station before I got through all the cars. He's probably out there some-where," I say, pointing to the train platform.

I grasp Grandma's arm. "So you saw him too?"

"I most certainly did, Agnes. That is until we entered that tunnel."

"That's why it got dark all of a sudden.

"So you believe he was following us?" I say.

"I do indeed."

"What are we going to do now?"

"I don't know how long we'll be here, but I'm guessin' he doesn't want te be found, after that disappearin' act," Grandma says.

Grandma turns me around and gently pushes me forward, her hands on both of my shoulders. "Let's finish our supper, girl, then we'll decide what to do. I'm not sure what I'm gonna say te those nice people we're eatin' with; they're very confused about why you ran out like that."

A

After we leave Dombås, we go through two more tunnels. The thought of going through a tunnel dug right through a mountain is pretty cool, but that's not the really cool part. Just before we enter the next tunnel, Georg brings out a compass and sets it on the table in between us.

"He likes this," Inger says and rolls her eyes like she thinks what he's doing is silly. I've seen that type of eye roll lots of times, but I'm a kid and Georg is an adult.

I might think taking out a compass while sitting in a train is silly too, until the dial on the compass starts to rotate. The train has slowed way down and has started to turn right. About half way into the turn, we duck into another tunnel. This time the electric lights go on inside the train car, and I can see that the compass is still turning.

"Do you know what that means?" Georg asks me, his eyes as bright as a child's on Christmas morning.

"We're going in a circle!" I say.

"That's right! Plus look at your water glass."

I had already noticed when we were eating dinner that the water wasn't level in the glasses on the table, but the water is at even more of an angle now. "We're going up. Cool!"

Once we're out of the tunnel, we make a wide left turn and pick up another river – the Gaula River. Georg's compass says we're heading northeast. Georg, who is a regular walking encyclopedia, tells me the Gaula is the longest river in Norway. He also tells me that we will go by the highest point in the Dovrefjell mountain range, Mount Snøhetta , which is 2286 meters high. I've seen three record points of interest in the trip so far: the largest lake, the longest river, and one of the highest peaks. This trip is starting to rank right up there with Istanbul.

A

It's almost midnight when Grandma nudges me awake.

"We're almost in Trondheim, Agnes. We have to get out here and wait for our next connection to Bodø."

Tales From the Arabian Nights falls from my lap as I sit up. Grandma and I read *To Kill a Mockingbird* to each other on the way to Norway and finished it by the time we got to Oslo, so we are both reading our new books. (I would definitely recommend

To Kill a Mockingbird if you want to read about a young girl who lives in the South and her creepy neighbors.) I didn't have time to finish all the *Arabian Nights* tales when we were in Istanbul, so I want to finish reading it.

If you think I forgot about our mystery man, you are mistaken. I thought about him all through dinner. And the more I thought about him, the more nervous I got. Maybe I shouldn't have ran after him. Maybe he's a dangerous man. My dad died under suspicious circumstances after all.

Once Grandma and I are alone again, I tell her what I'm thinking. She says that if we want to find out what really happened to my dad, we don't really have a choice; we have to follow every lead that comes our way. So after dinner we take our time and scour the length of the train, looking for the man with the steel-blue eyes and ugly tiepin, but we don't see hide nor hair of him. I guess he didn't get back on the train after I ran after him. I'm kind of glad we didn't find him because I was able to relax a bit more and read my book. I guess Grandma is right. The fact that he is following us has to have something to do with my dad. Why else would anyone care about a kid and an old lady traveling together? If we could have caught up with him, maybe we could have convinced him to tell us what really happened to my dad. My Grandma can be pretty convincing if she wants to be.

"How long do we have to wait?" I ask.

Grandma pulls out our tickets and looks at them. "Fifty minutes."

I pick up my book and look out the window. I notice that it's still light enough to see outside. I rub my eyes, thinking that maybe I'm still half asleep. I look at my wrist but my Mickey Mouse watch isn't there; Yusuf has it. I sure could use Yusuf's help about now, but my Grandma will have to do. I check Grandma Agee's watch and it's about ten minutes to eleven, even though it doesn't look like it out the train window. I cup my hands around my eyes and lean on the window so I can block out the light from inside the train car. It doesn't change a thing; it's still really weird looking outside; it's like time stood still while we were traveling. Everything looks a bit gray and fuzzy at the edges, but I can see the color and detail of all the houses and buildings we're passing by.

The train station is right on the water, which Georg tells me is the Trondheimsfjorden (*trond-himes-feeyoren*). Georg says that Norway is known for its fjords (*feeyores*) and when we come to visit again, we need to take a boat trip up one of them. He says it is quite a sight to see.

After I got up and ran after that man, Grandma told Georg and Inger how my dad died under strange circumstances, how we were told by the people he worked for – the US government, no less – that he died in Turkey but we think he really died right here in Bodø, Norway. Or at least that's the last place we know he was before he died. That's why we're here. Georg and Inger tell us they are getting out in Trondheim, but they wish us well on our search for the man from the Norwegian Intelligence Service. I'm disappointed they are leaving since talking to Georg is like having my own personal encyclopedia of Norway.

I am still not quite awake as we get our cases and stumble off the train with the rest of the drowsy passengers. Since we've got almost an hour wait, I convince Grandma to walk outside the train station so we can take a look around.

There is a wide walkway over top of the tracks that leads into the city, so we head for that. Grandma makes it to the edge of the walkway, just before a wide set of steps down into the city, and she sits down on our cases.

"I'll watch the cases, Agnes, if you want to walk a bit farther, but mind the cars in the street."

I go down the steps and across the street. The only people I see are those picking up passengers from our train. Everything is so still and quiet; I think everyone else is asleep.

Across the street is a river and rows of plain-looking, four- and five-story buildings painted red, green, orange, and off-white, all built right next to each other and right up next to the water. All the colors are dull now as the sky slowly darkens, but it makes me wonder why it's still so light out at eleven at night.

I lean on a railing that runs along the water and look at all the motor boats and sailboats in their slips along the river's edge. If you're wondering what a slip is, that's a nautical [*adj: of or related to sailors, navigation, or ships*] term for a place people park their boats in the water. A slip has piers on both sides of the boat, where a dock has a pier on only one side. I know nautical terms because my dad has...well, my mom now has a fishing boat. It used to be my dad's, of course, and he'd take me and my brothers fishing on the river during the summer and fall (on the Mississippi, of course). He couldn't take all of us at once, it wasn't that big of a boat. And we didn't leave it in a slip or tied to a pier on the river; we would take it in and out of the water anytime we were going fishing or if we just wanted to take a ride on the river. The boats on this river aren't fishing boats, though. They look more like boats to just go for a drive in or maybe go skiing behind. There are some of those on the Mississippi too, but mostly fishing boats.

Thinking about the boats and my dad, makes me sad, so I turn to go back across the street when I notice a man in a black suit and black cap get out of the car that is parked across the street in front of the station. Georg and Inger walk out of what must be the building people go into to buy train tickets because it says "NSB" in red above the doors. That is the initials of the Norway train system. I start to lift my hand to wave goodbye but they aren't looking at me; they're looking at the man in the black suit. He clicks his heels together as he opens the back door to the car for them to get into. Once they are in the car, he takes their cases and puts them in the trunk and they drive off. Seeing my new Norway friends leave makes me even sadder since I know Georg would have been a big help to Grandma and me in Bodø, though I'm sure the map he gave me will come in handy.

Grandma and I walk back over the walkway to the train platform, and we sit and wait on hard benches for our train to arrive. Grandma and I are so tired and sore by the time the train arrives, we head right for our sleeping car.

Chapter Six

Grandma and I both sleep very soundly until the next morning. The click clack of the wheels on the track and gentle rocking of the train easily lulls us to sleep. Not that we needed any help. Neither of us had slept well in the Amsterdam airport the night before, so I think we were asleep even before our heads hit our pillows, as my mother would say. In fact, Grandma is still in her nightgown when she wakes me.

"Agnes, we're almost there. We need to get up and get a move on," Grandma says as she reaches over her bed to gently shake me. Our sleeper looks like a small room with seats on each side, a door on one side and the window on the other. When you want to sleep, the porter (in our case it was a woman) unhooks a couple hidden latches and the seats pop up to become two small beds right next to each other. It's pretty ingenious, really. [Ingenious is an adjective that means *to be very clever.*]

It takes me a while to wake up. To be truthful, I don't want to wake up. I was having a dream about my dad. We were sitting along the river, fishing. My younger brothers were along too, but they had gotten bored and were playing in the rocks along the shore. My brothers were trying to get me wet and since there was two of them and only one of me, they were winning. I was complaining to my dad, asking him how I stop them from bothering me, and he told me to just stop fighting back. "They're only doing it to get a rise out of you," he said.

"But I don't have any choice; they'll win if I stop."

"You always have a choice, Agnes."

I prop myself up on my elbows and my eyes go wide. Grandma is looking in her suitcase for something to wear, and her hair, which is normally rolled up in a bun at the base of her neck, looks like a silvery river cascading [*v: to fall in or as if in a cascade: a steep usually small waterfall*] over her shoulders and down her back. Usually you'd use the word cascading for water that was flowing over rocks in a stream, but it fits perfectly here. Grandma's hair goes all the way down to the middle of her back, and I can tell she just took it out of her braid because it has waves all the way down to the end. I had seen her braid before, in Istanbul, but I had never seen her hair out of the braid. Seeing long hair on an old person is kind of like seeing one of my brothers in hair rollers, so I can't help but stare.

And as if she's self-conscious about her beautiful, long hair, she immediately and expertly braids it back up and rolls it into its usual bun.

"What you gawkin' at, girl? Get down here and get dressed. I must not a wound my alarm clock enough and I overslept, so we'll have to get breakfast once we're off the train. We're almost in the station, so get crackin'!"

I hurry up and change, then open the shade covering our window and what do I see but more water. Norway seems to be just mountains and water.

A

When we step off the train, I can't see the water anymore, so we must have traveled inland a bit. We grab a quick breakfast in the long, two-story train station. Grandma explains that we're not in

Bodø quite yet, we're in a small town called Fauske. Fauske is as far north as the train goes, though I can see from the work going on outside the station and the poster inside that they are planning on taking the train all the way to Bodø. I can read the year "1962" and "Bodø" on the poster along with some smiling passengers and a sleek, clean train – unlike the old one we just got off of – but that is all I can understand.

There is a row of long buses outside the station, so we pay our fare and get on one going to Bodø for the hour or so trip. It's a bright morning and the sun reflects off the water to our left for most of our bus ride (more fjords, according to my new map) with trees, hills, and mountains to our right. Bodø is on a peninsula right next to the ocean. I didn't bring a swimming suit – the thought of swimming never entered my mind – but I would at least like to dip my toes in the ocean, just to say I did it. With the sun streaming in the windows and my stomach pleasantly full, I doze off in the warm bus. Before I know it, I wake up yelling.

"Agnes, what's the matter, child?"

I squint at the bright sun and try and wake up from the dream I just fell out of. When I eventually do, I remember why I was yelling.

"Dad's letter!" I say to Grandma Agee.

"What?"

"The letter I was reading on the plane to France; Dad's last letter to you." I grab hold of Grandma's arm and hold on, willing her to understand me.

"What about it?"

"How did the man with the ugly tiepin know it was a letter?"

"What do you mean? He looked at it when he picked it up off the floor."

"It was underneath him, and before he even picked it up, he apologized for crushing Dad's letter."

Grandma looks at me sideways, like I am making this up. "Are you sure, girl?"

"I'm positive. He fell on it on purpose. He wanted to see that letter."

"But why?"

I sit back in my seat, the whole incident running in a loop through my brain. "I don't know."

A

In Bodø we pull up next to at least five other buses. When we get out, I see that we're just a couple short blocks from the water. But before we can start exploring, Grandma wants to find a place to stay, so we can get rid of our cases.

I look to our right, and there on the corner, just across the street, is the Norrona Hotell, the hotel sign propped up on the roof five stories up. (And yes, hotell is spelled with two Ls. That must be how they spell it in Norwegian.) There are five flags, including an American flag, hanging from flagpoles placed evenly above the windows on the first floor.

"How about there?" I say.

Grandma looks to where I'm pointing, picks up her suitcase, and heads across the street.

We step inside and the lobby is no bigger than my living room at home. There is a young couple talking with a young girl, who is behind the tall front desk. They are speaking something that sounds like Norwegian but not quite like what I've heard others in the country speaking. We set our cases down and wait our turn. A man about my dad's age comes to take the room key for the couple and both of their suitcases and they follow him out of the lobby.

When we step up to the desk, the young girl is still standing there. I kind of figured an adult would be taking her place, but I was wrong. She can't be any older than me. I wonder why she's working here.

"Kan jeg hjelpe deg?"

Neither Grandma nor I understand her, but Grandma just plows ahead anyway. "We need a room for two," she says, pointing to me then herself. I guess she figures the pantomiming [*v. a way of expressing information or telling a story without words by using body movements and facial expressions*] will help if the girl only speaks Norwegian, and in such a small town, so far up north, I would guess that would be the case.

"Of course," the girl says in English, "a room for two."

She turns around and pulls a key off of a rack of keys and numbers on a large board behind her. She sets it on the counter. As Grandma fills out the required paperwork, I notice another girl, I'd say she's about fifteen or sixteen, sitting in one of the three lobby chairs against the wall. She has a folded paper in her hand and a pencil, and she's writing something down on the paper every minute or so. I walk over and sit next to her to see if I can tell what she's doing.

She stands up the minute I sit down, so I don't get to see what she's doing. But she doesn't move too far; she leans up against the wall and continues working on her paper project.

"Janne (Ya-nna)," the girl at the desk calls over. "Rom 418."

Now I know the girl isn't sitting in the lobby because she is waiting for someone, she works here too, even though she doesn't have on any kind of uniform like Baris did at the Hotel Zanzibar in Istanbul.

Janne sets her paper and pencil down on the small table next to the chair she was sitting in, and I can see that she was working on a crossword puzzle. I smile at her, knowing we'll get along just swell since she's a lover of words like I am. I do the crossword in our paper every Sunday. The funny thing about Janne is, though, she doesn't look at me at all. Well, that's not quite right; she sees me, but she doesn't turn her face up to look at me. She looks at me out of the corner of her eyes, like her neck doesn't move to let her look up. That makes me wonder if she was in some sort of accident, or maybe she just woke up with a crick in her neck and the problem is temporary.

Janne goes over to our cases, picks up one in each hand, then walks out of the room.

"Janne, husk å vente," the girl at the desk says and Janne stops just outside the lobby door.

I still have my shoulder-bag on, so I put my Pan

Am bag over my other shoulder and follow Grandma Agee out. Janne turns before we get close to her and without saying a thing, walks over to a narrow stairwell and starts to walk up. Grandma and I look at each other and both shrug our shoulders at the same time. At least I'm not the only one who thinks Janne seems a bit different.

Janne struggles a bit with both cases and after the second set of steps, Grandma can't help herself, she has to say something. "Can I take one of those, my dear?"

Janne stops and turns on the landing but, again, doesn't lift her face to look at us when she speaks. "No," is all she says, and she continues on up the next flight while we slowly plod along behind her.

We meet the young couple that just went up, coming down partway along the third flight of stairs. Janne hears them coming and rushes to the middle landing and plasters herself into one of the corners, avoiding eye contact until they noisily walk by chatting to themselves, then she moves on up to the third floor.

At room 418, Janne sets our cases down, opens the door, and puts our cases in the room. Just like Baris, she opens the bathroom door, but there is no balcony in this room, so she heads back out of the room without stopping for a tip.

"Wait," Grandma calls to her and follows her out. I follow out too.

Grandma reaches out to give her a dollar and just before Grandma is about to place it into her hand, the girl moves her hand and the dollar floats to the floor. Janne quickly squats down to pick it up as if she wants to get to it before my grandmother does. Then without looking at either of us, she says a muffled "Thank you" in very understandable English, and she practically runs down the hall and down the stairwell.

"Well, if that don't beat all," Grandma Agee says.

I have to agree with her. That's when I know there's more wrong with Janne than a sore neck.

The room is neat and a bit wider than the room at the Zanibar in Istanbul. It has the same two twin beds and a small nightstand between them, but this room has a small desk in one corner and two upholstered chairs with a two-foot-square table between them.

I go to the double windows on the other side of the room and look out. We are just three blocks from the water, and I have a clear view of a large bay. Straight across are two islands, the farthest one much bigger and taller than the other. I dig out my map of Norway. On the back side of the map of the country are smaller maps of major cities: Oslo, Bergen, Trondheim, Bodø, and Vadso are just a few of them. The map of Bodø tells me the taller island is 131 meters at its highest point. From out the window it doesn't look like there is anyone living on the islands, but there are a few buildings on the thin peninsula that creates the large bay in front of the town.

"So where do you want to go first?" I ask.

Grandma Agee sits on the bed and doesn't say anything for a few seconds. "That's a good question."

Grandma moves over to my bed and looks at the city map. "Bodø is smaller than I thought it might be. I wonder why your father was working here."

"Do you think the Norwegian Intelligence Service has an office in Bodø somewhere?"

"I don't know, but that would be a good place to start."

Grandma goes to the desk and pulls open the small drawer but it's empty. "No phone directory."

I look around the room. "No phone!"

"I guess we'll have to go by shank's mare, then," Grandma says as she picks up her purse.

"Huh?"

"Go on foot," Grandma explains as she heads out the door.

I grab my shoulder-bag and follow her out.

When we get back to the lobby, the desk is empty and so is the lobby. Grandma rings the bell on the countertop, and less than a minute later a woman with graying hair appears. She smiles when she sees us.

"Hvordan kan jeg hjelpe deg?"

"Do you speak English?" Grandma says.

"Yes, of course. How may I help you?"

Just before Grandma can respond, two men in military uniforms walk through the main doors and set their cases down behind Grandma and me.

Grandma looks at the men, then at me like she's not quite sure how to respond to the woman at the desk, now that we're not the only ones in the room. I'm wondering too. Is she going to spill the whole story like she did to Georg and Inger or give the condensed version she gave to the woman at the embassy? I'm a little nervous after the man with the weird tiepin had been following us. I know he wasn't on the train to Trondheim, but he's put me on my guard, and I don't want Grandma to give too much away, just in case someone else would be following us.

"We're wonderin' if you might have a phone directory."

The woman pulls a thin phonebook out from under the desk and hands it to Grandma Agee. She takes the book and we sit in the lobby to look it over. While Grandma's paging through the book, the two military men step up to the counter.

"Hello Mrs. Iversen. The usual for Mr. Davis and myself."

My head pops up when I hear the man speak because they are definitely not from around here; they sound like I do. I notice the case that the man closest to me is holding. I recognize an emblem that I have in my own home: an American Air Force emblem. There is a picture hanging in the basement workshop of my dad in a jumpsuit in front of plane that has that emblem on it. In the picture my dad has a helmet under his arm as he stands on a ladder about to get into the cockpit of the plane.

My attention is drawn to Grandma Agee when she shuts the phonebook and sighs.

"No help?" I ask.

"This was about as useful as a screen door in a submarine."

I have to giggle at Grandma's little saying. I've never heard anything like that before. It doesn't sound like an idiom but it's kind of close, and I understand perfectly what she's trying to say.

"I might have an idea," I say, and I direct Grandma's attention to the two men standing at the desk. "They're in the Airforce, like Dad." I stop and catch myself. "Like Dad was."

Grandma puts her hand on my knee because she's made that same present tense mistake too. Then she sits at attention as she looks the two men over.

The woman at the desk hits the bell and Janne appears next to the woman. When they stand next to each other, I can tell they must be mother and daughter because they both have the same blondish-brown hair, though Janne's doesn't have any gray in it, of course. They dress alike too; the mom has on a sky-blue jumper and a white blouse and Janne has a red one. The mother says something to Janne in Norwegian and gives her two keys. Janne goes around the counter and heads toward the stairs, not trying to pick up the cases like she did for Grandma and me. The men follow as if they've done this before.

When they turn, I can tell one man is an officer by all the salad he has on his chest. "Salad" is what Dad called the medals a military man has on his chest. My dad had a bit of "salad" himself; I saw it on a picture my mom has on her dresser in their room.

Well...now it's just her room. I know he has a Purple Heart because he got wounded a couple times, but I don't know what all the other colored bars and pins mean. I'll have to ask Mom when I get home. Or maybe Grandma even knows.

As they leave, the younger girl that was manning the desk when we first came in walks into the room and sits down in the chair next to me. I'm not sure why I should say she was "manning" the desk because she's not a man working at a desk, she's a woman, or to be more correct, she's a girl about my age, but girling the desk doesn't sound right. I only have the travel dictionary mom gave me for the trip so I'll have to look at my thesaurus when I get home and find a better word for manning.

The girl picks up the crossword puzzle and one of three pencils that are sitting neatly on the small table next to the chairs and starts working on it. She has a jumper on too; hers is a navy-blue color. If she's related to Janne and her mom, she doesn't look like it. Her hair is brown, a shade lighter than her eyes. But she has the same crossword that Janne was working on, so I can't imagine a stranger would work on a puzzle that didn't belong to them. And not all of my siblings resemble [*v: to be like or similar*] each other, either. Dad, Aaron, and I have what Peggy describes as strawberry blond hair. I'm not sure why they call it that; it's nothing like the color of strawberries. It's more like the color of a red shirt that was washed one too many times. Adam and Max have Mom's dark brown hair color, so dark it almost looks black. Peter and Danny are blond. I'm not sure where that color came from, but I heard Uncle Bob say at Dad's funeral it must have come from the milk man. The people all around him laughed after he said it, but I don't know what was so funny.

I lean over and make it obvious to the girl that I'm looking at her puzzle. "I like crosswords too, but in English, of course."

"My sister, Janne, can do English puzzles. I can only do puzzles in Norwegian."

"Your sister must be pretty smart to know two languages. I only know one. Well, two, if you consider pig Latin a language."

"What is pig Latin?"

"It's not hard, really, once you know the trick. My older brother, Adam, thought he could use it to talk to his friends and I wouldn't understand, but I figured it out almost right away. I'll show you. Can I use your pencil?"

The girl looks at me as if I've asked to borrow

a million dollars. "They are my sister's pencils, and I'm the only one she lets use them."

"I won't steal it or anything. I just want to show you how pig Latin works."

She looks around the lobby then slowly hands me the pencil.

"Can I use the newspaper too?"

"Oh, no! That would not work." The girl jumps up and goes around the desk to find a scrap piece of paper in the trash. "Is this okay?" she asks, handing me the scrap.

"Um, sure." I take the paper and write a sentence twice, one the regular way, then the second in pig Latin:

The sun looks bright and hot.
E-thay un-say ooks-lay ight-bray nd-yay ot-hay.

"See what I did? I took the first letter or two of each word, put it on the back of the word and added ay."

The girl giggles. "That's very funny."

"For something like 'I' you'd just put 'yay' at the end: I-yay."

I write the word down and show her.

"Everyone in Norway knows Norwegian,

Swedish, and Dutch. They are very similar languages. We are taught English and German in school, but most adults aren't very good at those languages. My parents know English and some German because of running this hotel. We get a lot of English speakers who stay here because of the military base and some Brits too."

"Oh! That explains why most everyone we've talked to can speak English. Is British English different than American English?"

"The accent and some of the spelling is different, but it's basically the same."

"Does anyone come and stay here that works for the American CIA, the Central Intelligence Agency?" Grandma asks.

"Not that I know of. We mostly get American and British pilots or officers from other NATO countries that work at the air base."

Then as if to make the girl's point, we hear a loud roar above us. The sound builds in seconds, zooms overhead, and is gone just as fast. It is so loud Grandma and I duck slightly, like the plane would hit us if we didn't drop our heads. The girl doesn't flinch.

"The airfield is about three kilometers behind us," the girl says and points to her left.

"Trine, Jeg kommer til å hjelpe din far på kjøkkenet. Kom og se på skrivebordet, vennligst," Trine's mother says.

Trine (sounds like Tree-na) immediately gets up and puts her hand out for the pencil. I give it to her, and she puts the puzzle and pencil neatly on the small table, just like she found them, and takes her mother's place behind the desk.

"Another screen door, Grandma," I say, using her saying for not getting any useful information.

Trine leafs through the ledger in front of her. "But we do get members of the Etterretningstjenesten that stay here."

My head pops up. "What did you say?" I walk up to stand in front of the desk. Grandma Agee follows me.

"The Etterretningstjenesten is the Norwegian Intelligence Service, though everyone calls it E. for short. It is like your CIA."

I turn and whisper to Grandma, "Like E14!"

Grandma Agee nods and her eyes light up. They don't actually turn on like a flashlight or start on fire or anything. That's an idiom that means they look excited, and I can tell she's as happy about what we just heard as I am.

"We even have someone from the E. staying with us right now."

Trine turns the ledger around so we can see it. Right next to the date June 20 is the signature *N.W. Borge.*

Chapter Seven

Grandma and I smile at each other the same way Peggy and I did when we found out that we had both gotten A's on our final geography test. That screen door just turned into a sturdy metal hull or maybe just a seal-proof door; we still have to find Mr. Borge and talk to him, but now we know where he goes to sleep every night. This will be a cinch [*n: an easy thing to do, something sure to happen*].

Someone had placed a capital E behind Mr. Borge's name in pencil. I notice the two airmen we saw earlier have a capital A behind their signatures.

"Is Mr. Borge here?" I ask.

"No, he left right after breakfast."

"For the air base?" Grandma says.

"I don't know, but that would be my guess."

Grandma rustles through her purse and pulls out her wallet. "Would ya mind calling a taxi? I think these old legs aren't up to walkin' three kilometers anymore.

"Of course."

Trine pulls out a small directory and starts paging through it.

As Grandma and I look at each other, a man in an American Air Force uniform steps into the lobby from outside.

He walks up to the counter, and Grandma and I move out of his way. "The ride for Colonel Wagner and Lieutenant Davis is here."

Grandma and I look at each other and we both get a conspiratorial smile on our faces. If you remember from my Istanbul story, to conspire is *to agree secretly to do an unlawful act*. We're not going to do anything against the law, any more than Bubbles – my mom's nickname with she was a kid – and my mom's childhood friend Jane would do on the school playground, but I think Grandma and I have the same idea about a ride to the air base.

"I will let them know when they come down," Trine tells the man.

He turns and leaves. I walk over to the entrance

doors and watch the man get into a small, blue car. Many of the cars in Bodø are compact. They remind me of Max's matchbox cars.

"Trine, never mind about the taxi," Grandma Agee says.

Grandma pushes open one of the hotel entrance doors and waves for me to follow. When I stand next to her, she grabs hard onto my arm and takes one step at a time down the small set of steps. This is strange because Grandma doesn't usually have any difficulty with steps.

"What's the matter, Grandma?"

"Nothin' child. Just play along," she whispers.

She doesn't let go of me as she directs me over to the small, blue car.

She taps on the window. The car is narrow so the man easily reaches over to the passenger side door and rolls the window down.

"Are you going to the air base, young man?" Grandma asks.

"Yes ma'am."

"My granddaughter and I have a meetin' at the air base, but we have no way to get there. Would you mind helpin' an old lady out and givin' us a ride?"

"I'm not authorized, ma'am. I'm here to pick up a couple passengers."

"Is there a problem here?"

We both turn and see two men in military uniforms standing behind us, the same two men that had checked in just moments ago. Grandma and I were focused on the man in the car, and we didn't hear Colonel Wagner and the Lieutenant Davis walk up behind us.

The man in the car gets out so he can face the colonel. "These folks are looking for a ride to the air base, Colonel."

Colonel Wagner furrows his brow, looks at me, then at Grandma Agee. "You have business at the air base?"

"Yes we do."

"With whom?"

Grandma looks at me and I can see the thoughts running through her head: *Do I tell this man who we're trying to find? Do I fill him in on what happened to Patrick, why we've traveled halfway around the globe to be here?*

She turns back to the colonel. "We are meeting with a Mr. Borge of EI4."

There is a sudden panicked look on the colonel's face. Both he and the lieutenant step closer to us and look up and down the street as if we are suddenly in imminent danger.

"Get in the car," Colonel Wagner commands and pushes us back toward the back door of the little blue car.

Lieutenant Davis opens the back door and Grandma and I are unceremoniously ushered into the back seat (that means we're basically pushed inside). The lieutenant sees that there really isn't any more room for him so he stands outside our door. The Colonel notices as well.

"I'll send the car back for you, Lieutenant."

"Very well, sir," he says with a curt nod and steps away from the car. Curt is a fun word because it sounds just like its definition: *said or done in a quick and impolite way.*

Colonel Wagner and the driver get in and speed off down the street.

Now we feel like we're back in the taxi in Istanbul on our trip to the blue mosque; the driver turns corners and makes stops as if the back of the car is on fire. But Grandma doesn't hit this man like she did the taxi driver in Istanbul, she just holds tightly onto me and the small arm rest on the door. She looks as baffled [*adj: confused*] by the sudden turn of events as I am.

It takes less than ten minutes and we're pulling up to a guard box in front of the air base. There is a large Royal Norwegian Air force seal on the guard box – a bird with *Luftforsvaret* written under it (and something else I can't read) and a crown above it. The guard has on a Norwegian uniform. There are also two soldiers holding guns on each side of the wooden guardrail that bars vehicles from driving into the base.

"Colonel Wagner...and guests," the driver says to the guard.

The guard looks in the back seat but doesn't seem sure of what to do. "It's fine, private. I'll take responsibility," the colonel says.

The private steps away from the car and salutes. He signals to one of the gun-toting soldiers standing by the wooden guardrail. The pole floats up and we drive onto the air base.

When we get out of the car, I can see that we're on the opposite side of the civilian airport. Across the runway are commercial jets and small prop planes like the ones we took to get to Oslo. On this side there are military hangers and military planes of different shapes and sizes lined up next to the runway. Most of them look alike, other than the emblem of the country they belong to on their sides or their tails. But there is one plane that isn't sitting out with the rest; it's in an open upside down, U-shaped airplane hangar. It's not like any of the other planes in that it is completely black, a lot smaller, and has really long wings, so long in fact that it has poles under the tips of the wings, holding them up.

"This way, ladies," the colonel says, directing us to a small, two-story building in front of us. As we get closer to the door, our attention is drawn to a small plane that roars past us on the runway and, as if launched from a giant, invisible rubber band, soars off into the clear blue sky until it's no more than a speck on the horizon.

"One of our F4s," Colonel Wagner explains as he opens the door for us and waits for us to go inside. We step past another soldier that is holding a gun. The gun looks like one of my dad's hunting rifles. I know he's not waiting for a white tail deer to come strolling by, but I can't help but wonder what or who he is waiting for.

The colonel walks us past the male receptionist in a military shirt and tie and down a long hall. He opens a door and directs us to enter. There is a rectangular metal table in the room with an empty glass ashtray sitting in the middle and four metal chairs around it but nothing else, not even a window.

"Have a seat, please," he says in a very business-like voice. It's the same tone my mother uses in church when my brothers are monkeying around.

He then closes the door and both Grandma and I hear the lock click into place.

I lean over to Grandma. "What's going on?"

Grandma goes over to test the door. She tries to turn the handle but it doesn't budge.

She turns back to me. "I have no idea."

A

It takes a good thirty minutes before we hear the door lock click open and see the young man that was sitting at the reception desk in the doorway.

"If you ladies would please follow me."

Grandma Agee stands but doesn't leave the table. "Listen, young man, we're not going anywhere until we find out why we're bein' held here." I stand too, in solidarity with my grandmother. I learned the word solidarity from the newspaper, when I was reading about some white students in Louisiana who were sitting at a soda fountain counter with some black students. Sitting at a soda fountain is not a big deal, of course, but the paper said they were sitting in solidarity with their black friends, because the black students weren't allowed to sit there, like the black people riding the bus with the white people, I guess. I didn't know what the word was until I looked it up [*n: a feeling of unity between people who have the same interests, goals, etc.*] and I think it fits in this situation perfectly. Grandma and I are in this together now, so we have to look out for each other. Before this trip, if you would have told me I'd be standing up for a lady who I don't really know and who is some fifty years older than me, I'd have said you needed to get your head examined. But Grandma and I are on a mission, and whatever happens, we're in this together.

"I'm not at liberty to say, ma'am."

"Then find someone who is," Grandma says in a tone that obviously means business. Then she sits back down and stares at me until I sit too.

The young man opens his mouth like he's going to start arguing with my grandmother, but when she gives him a look he's probably seen from his own grandmother, he closes his mouth and then the door, locking us back in.

I don't know where Grandma gets her guts from because I'm shaking in my boots, or more accurately, in my saddle shoes. I'd have followed the young man out of the room, no questions asked. Putting us in this room is just like in those detective books I read. The private eye locks the bad guy in a room with no windows for hours upon hours, making the guy sweat, and by the time the private eye comes back to talk to the bad guy, he is ready to tell the private eye all he wants to know. I know we haven't been in this room for hours, but it sure feels like it. I'm not sure what it was that Grandma said to the colonel that has gotten us into so much trouble, but something sure has. I thought we were in trouble when we had that man with the funny tiepin follow us, but now it seems like we're in trouble with our own government too.

This time it's just a few minutes and Colonel Wagner steps into the room. Grandma Agee and I automatically stand.

"Mrs. Kelly, if you and your granddaughter would follow me, we'll explain why I've brought you here."

Mrs. Kelly? Mrs. Kelly! How does he know my grandmother's name? And how does he know I'm her granddaughter?

I search my grandmother's face to see if she's as shocked as I am, but she's as cool as a cucumber, as my dad would say. I'm not sure exactly why a cucumber is considered cool, and I'm not talking about the same "cool" I usually mean when I say that word. Being cool as a cumber must have something to do with temperature or maybe it's the taste, but I'm really not sure. At my house Mom either makes pickles out of cucumbers in a big crock in our basement, or she cuts them up and puts a white sauce over them; both taste disgusting to me – not sour exactly or bitter, just not good.

Grandma doesn't say anything, she just follows Colonel Wagner out of the room and so do I.

The next room we are taken to has the same metal table and chairs, but this one has a window in it, though the shade is pulled closed. There are two men in the room who stand as we walk in. One of the men is tall and thin, the other is short and wears glasses. The man with the glasses is smoking a cigarette, and he mashes it in a glass ashtray identical to the one in the room we just left. It takes me a few seconds but I know who the tall man is, and I stop as if my feet are stuck in cement.

TOP SECRET

Chapter Eight

My heart is racing and I don't know what to do. The man with the steely-blue eyes is standing next to the short man with glasses. With the blue-eyed man in the room, I know for sure we're in trouble, but I'm not sure how to get us out of it. So I do the first thing that comes to me: I kick Colonel Wagner in the shin, grab grandma's arm, and hightail it out of the room. They don't expect us to flee, so we have the element of surprise on our side, and it takes them a moment to react.

"Run! Run, Agnes!" I hear my grandma yell from behind me. We run down the hall with the men in hot pursuit. We run past the receptionist before he realizes what's going on. My heart is beating so fast

I can feel its thump, thump, thump in my ears. We push through the front doors, and the bright sun blinds us momentarily.

Okay, I didn't just kick the colonel in the shin; I imagined it in my head. But as I run the plan through to its ultimate [*adj: arrived at as the last result*] conclusion, I realize if we did happen to outrun these men (and that's questionable pulling along a sixty-some-year-old grandmother) and we made it out of the building, those soldiers standing around with guns in their hands surely wouldn't let us get very far.

I look over at my grandmother to see if she recognizes the blue-eyed man, but she doesn't seem to. When I think about it, why would she; she's only seen him once, on the Air France plane four days ago. His haircut was different then. She didn't see him in the train station in Oslo, and she didn't get a good look at him on the train to Bodø like I did. She got a glimpse of him before the lights went out but that's all. It's the new haircut and those steel-blue eyes that give him away to me – he ditched the ugly tiepin somewhere since he's got just a regular straight one on now. Then I wonder again why someone would be following my grandma and me all the way from Istanbul? And why would he be here?

I try and get Grandma's attention, clearing my

throat and nodding my head in his direction when she looks over at me, but she doesn't understand; she sits down in one of the two chairs that are being pulled out for us.

I don't know the man with the glasses, who is shaped kind of like a pear – big on the bottom and small on the top – until he comes over to Grandma Agee and introduces himself.

"Mrs. Kelly, I'm Nikolia Borge. I believe you've been looking for me."

It takes Grandma a minute to speak. "Mr. Borge? Why...why are you on this military base?"

The man looks amused [*v: to please your sense of humor – to think something is funny*]. "I think I could ask you that same question."

Grandma looks at Colonel Wagner, then back at Mr. Borge. "I think you know why we're here."

Mr. Borge looks at the man who has been following us, then pulls out a chair and sits back down.

"All right, Mrs. Kelly. We can drop all pretense here. You know I'm a member of EI4, but I suspect you don't have any idea what EI4 is."

"I know you have somethin' to do with my Patrick's death. That's all I need te know."

Mr. Borge closes his eyes for a second and takes a deep breath. "Mrs. Kelly, I had nothing to do with your son's death."

"Then why was he in Norway meeting you just before he died?"

"Why would your son be in Norway? He sold insurance for the US government."

Now my grandma looks annoyed. "I thought you were going to drop the pretense, Mr. Borge. I know Patrick worked for the CIA, not because he told me. He hasn't told anyone." Grandma shakes her head and corrects herself. "He didn't tell anyone. I figured that out myself, though I am not going to disclose just how. Anyway, he sent me a letter postmarked from Bodø, Norway just before he died, so I know he was here, not in Turkey as we were told."

Mr. Borge stiffens at this. Colonel Wagner leans over and whispers something in his ear. Mr. Borge frowns and whispers something back.

"Go ahead, then," Colonel Wagner finally says out loud.

Mr. Borge sighs then speaks. "Yes, your son works...*worked* for the CIA."

I notice that Mr. Borge is having the same trouble with the past tense thing we are.

"But I can assure you, he wasn't in Norway when he...died."

"Then how do you explain his letter?"

"EI4 is a branch of the Etterretningstjenesten,

the Norwegian Intelligence Service." Mr. Borge looks at Colonel Wagner before he goes on. "It's supposed to be a covert branch, so when you mentioned it at the embassy in Oslo, well, naturally we were quite alarmed."

I knew that woman at the embassy was ratting on us!

Grandma doesn't respond to this bit of news, so I know she's as surprised as I am.

"The United States and Norway are North Atlantic Treaty Organization allies – NATO allies, so it's not unusual for your son to work with the Etterretningstjenesten."

"What could the CIA possibly be doing with EI4?"

Colonel Wagner answers Grandma's question. "That's top secret information, Mrs. Kelly, and not something we can share. The operation is still ongoing."

The colonel walks over to Grandma Agee and sits on the edge of the table. He lowers his voice as if someone is listening on the other side of the door. "The fate of the United States, not to mention our global partners such as Norway, Turkey, and even your home country of Ireland would be put at risk if such information were to get out. Your son knew that too. That's why he was willing to put himself at risk for his country. He should be commended for using his unique skills as an operative for our country."

"But you can't because no one can know what he was doin'?" Grandma says so softly it's like she's saying it to herself.

"Exactly."

"You seem to know a lot about us, Mr. Wagner, so you know we are not a threat. You could have told his wife what happened to Patrick. You could have told me."

"We had no choice, Mrs. Kelly."

Grandma shakes her head. "You always have a choice, Colonel."

I stare at Grandma. *That's just what Dad said to me in my dream!*

Mr. Borge pulls an envelope out of his pocket, sets it on the table, and shoves it toward Grandma Agee.

"We know you and your granddaughter have come a long way, Mrs. Kelly, so we've arranged for your flight back to the United States," he says with a big smile on his face. "We assume you prefer to escort Agnes back to her family versus heading home to Ireland. The flight isn't scheduled until Wednesday morning, so you have a full day to enjoy this lovely seaside town before you leave. Unfortunately you'll miss our Midsummer Night celebration on the twenty-third. We have many community bonfires to enjoy the midnight sun. I don't know if you've noticed, but above the Arctic Circle the sun doesn't set from mid-May through July."

So that's why it was so light outside at eleven at night in Trondheim, I think.

The room is silent as Grandma stares at the envelope, so all eyes turn toward me when my stomach decides to tell the room that it hasn't been fed in a while.

I clutch my middle and turn a bright shade of pink as most everyone in the room chuckles softly. Even Grandma cracks a small smile.

Mr. Borge stands, picks up the envelope on the table, and tries to hand it to my grandmother. "Please, Mrs. Kelly. If you won't take it for yourself, take it for your son's child."

Grandma reluctantly takes the envelope. Mr. Borge walks over to the door and opens it. "I'm sorry we've kept you so long. I'll have the driver take you to Monty's. Bodø is famous for its wonderful seafood, and Monty's has the finest."

Grandma and I stand.

"I'll call ahead and get you a table," he says as he puts his arm around my shoulders as if we're close chums, then he escorts us out of the room. "And remember, what you have heard here cannot be shared with anyone, not even your daughter-in-law. It would put people you love and care about at risk, and you wouldn't want to do that, would you?"

When Grandma doesn't answer, I figure his question is what grownups call rhetorical, which means it's a question not really looking for an answer. Another silly thing adults made up. Go figure.

Chapter Nine

Dear Peggy,

A lot has happened since I last wrote to you. Sorry it's taken me so long to write, but there is a lot to see in Norway, and I was hoping I'd have some better news to share.

It turns out that ⇄✓&★⑥❀✓ ▤★〰↔🗁 was not in Oslo but in a small town above the Arctic Circle called Bodø. (I can't use his real name anymore because he is part of a secret Norwegian organization.) Grandma decided since we came all this way, we might as well go to Bodø too. But Bodø is a long way from Oslo, so it took us two days on a train to get here.

You'd think being above the Arctic Circle

would mean it would be really cold here, but it isn't. It's not as warm as back home, but I can wear a light jacket or a sweater and be just fine. The other cool thing about being above the Arctic Circle is that in June and July the sun never really sets. It gets close to the horizon but it never goes below it. How cool is that! That means it's light twenty-four hours a day. The sky isn't light-blue for twenty-four hours, it turns a blue-gray color at night with an orange horizon, but it never gets dark. It's really kind of weird. I know all this because we made friends on the train with a really nice couple by the name of Georg and Inger. They got off at a town called Trondheim, so they didn't come with us to Bodø. They gave me a map of their country, so I'll be able to show you in detail everywhere we went.

Believe it or not, we did end up finding Mr. ▤. It was quite by accident, really. And you can't tell anyone, but he works for ⇇★∿^📭↔✓❀⇇ ✓⇇=📭⑥⑥✓↔📭⇇◆📭 ☺📭∿❖✓◆📭 in a what he called a covert branch. I looked up covert after our meeting with him. It means made, shown, or done in a way that is not easily seen or noticed: secret or hidden. It turns out my dad was not only working for the ◆✓❀, he *was also working with the ⇇✓☺. That's why his last letter to my grandmother was from Norway. When we met Mr. ▤., we also met a man who was ☺△%✓⇇↔ on us most of the way here. I think Mr. ▤ and this other man must have been working together, but I'm not sure, and to be honest, I was too scared to ask. I didn't know governments could be so sneaky. And like my grandma said, why would they care that Grandma and I were trying to find out what happened to my dad?*

I'm sitting in bed writing to Peggy. I stop writing to burp, and all I taste is fish.

I have to admit, the huge hunk of fish I ate at Monty's tasted pretty good. The menu said it was halibut. I'm no stranger to fish, but I've never had halibut before. I've eaten mostly blue gills and crappies with an occasional walleye or catfish, depending on what is in season. We'd get these out of the river or a lake close by De Soto with the boring name of Big Lake, which is really just a shallow backwater lake in the Mississippi. And the fish at Monty's had a fancy sauce on it that spiced it up a bit, but it still tasted pretty good.

Grandma was going to try lutefisk (*lu-ta-fisk*), which is a Norwegian fish dish, but the waiter

thought she would like the smoked salmon better –
it's called laks (*luxs*) here in Norway – and we both
ate everything on our plate. After what happened to
us today, I could have eaten a piece of shoe leather.
Well, I'm exaggerating a bit, but both Grandma and
I were pretty hungry. Norwegian food seems a bit
more like American food compared to the things
we ate in Istanbul. We had boiled potatoes with
our fish, a lettuce salad, and some cheese. The only
thing I didn't eat was the cheese. It was caramel-
colored and looked like it had sat out too long. I
live in a state that's known for its cheese and I've
never seen brown cheese before, so I left it all for
Grandma. She liked it!

Besides them paying for our flight home, our
meal was paid for too, which made Grandma very
happy. For a short while, anyway. We still didn't find
out how my dad died or why, so I'm not sure if we
are totally safe yet. I sure would like to know what
happened to him, and from how quiet Grandma
Agee was at dinner, I know she wanted to find out
too. I had imagined the look on my family's faces
when I told them that Dad really worked for the
CIA and that he died protecting our country. But
we can't tell anyone anything, not even my mom.
It's top secret. But what was my dad doing that got

him into trouble? Did his death mean anything to anyone but our family? I guess we'll never know. My handkerchief is in my shoulder-bag, so I use the blanket to wipe the tears from my eyes. But the bigger question is, are we in danger now?

Grandma is in bed reading her Hawaii book while I'm writing to Peggy. I'm disappointed we couldn't find out anything about what my dad was doing before he died, but I'm proud to know he was working to keep our country safe, or at least that is what they told us.

But now it's all water under the bridge, as the grownups say, and we're heading home soon. Mr. 🗎. was nice enough to buy our plane tickets for us, so I'll be seeing you soon. I'll fill you in on all the details, as long as you promise to keep it a secret, I mean like cross your heart and hope to die, secret!

Your best friend,
Agnes

The next morning, Trine is our waitress at breakfast. As I watch her scurry around the restaurant, I think that maybe kids in other countries work harder than kids in the US. You don't see kids in the US selling scarves to tourists outside of churches, even though ladies are supposed to wear something on their heads in Catholic churches too. And I haven't been in many restaurants, but I've never seen a girl as young as Trine working in a restaurant back home. Janne looks like she'd be old enough to be a waitress, but she's nowhere to be seen.

"Good morning," Trine says as she puts a basket of bread and a small jar of red-colored jam on the table. "Would you like coffee or tea?"

"Coffee would be wonderful," Grandma Agee says.

"Do you have orange juice?" I ask. I haven't had orange juice in a long time so that sounds really good to me.

Trine shakes her head. "Apple juice."

"Okay."

I look around the restaurant again but still don't see Janne. "Is your sister at the front desk?"

"Janne is in the kitchen. She doesn't like to be around people much. She only helps at the front if my pappa is busy."

A

After Trine brings us our drinks, she takes our order and I try another question.

"I would like to buy a postcard for my family, and I have a letter to mail. Is there somewhere in town I can do those things?"

"Of course. You can get the postcard at the AGA right next door, and I can take you to the post office after everyone is done with their breakfast."

I look over at Grandma Agee and give her my best *Sound okay to you?* expression.

"That would be fine," she says. "I'll read my book in the lobby until you get back. Then we can stroll down to the water and look around town."

"My sister and I would be happy to show you around. Tuesdays are not very busy for us, so we have more free time. Janne can drive now, so she could take us to wherever you want to go. Many tourists go to Saltstraumen. It is north of Bodø. This is where you can see the world's strongest tidal currents. Or we could show you some German bunkers from the war. Germany occupied all of Norway during the war, and because of our airport and our port, they had many fortifications around the city. There is also the Nyholmen Skandse ruins on the peninsula across the bay. It was a military fort a long time ago."

"You sound like you'd be a wonderful guide," my grandma says.

"It is Janne who knows all about these things.

She can remember anything she's read. Mamma says it's a special gift."

A

After we are through with breakfast, we go back up to our room. I grab my bag and my letter. Grandma decides she wants to send a letter to Uncle Bob telling him we struck out. He was the only one of her nine...now eight kids who knew my dad worked for the CIA, so he's the only one she can talk to about it. I found out at the funeral that Uncle Bob had moved back to live with Grandma Agee about six months ago, after he got divorced. Uncle Bob was in the war, just like my dad, but he was in the British Army; Grandma said Ireland didn't have its own army during WWII.

"Should I wait until you're done with your letter so I can mail it for you?"

"Go get your post card, then come back and we'll go to the post together."

Grandma sits down at the small desk and pulls a hotel notepad out of the desk drawer. "You've still got a few kroner left from the train station, don't ya?"

"Yup. I should be good."

I scurry down the four flights of stairs and pop

into the lobby. Janne is sitting doing her crossword but no one else is around. I step up to her, and she does that same thing with her head: she looks at me with her eyes but doesn't lift her head to face me. I bend down to look at her better, and she buries her chin in her chest. I give up and just stand up straight.

"Do you know where your sister is?"

She shakes her head.

"Can you give her a message for me?"

Janne looks at me again, without lifting her head, then nods in the affirmative (you can probably figure out what that word means).

"Tell her my grandmother and I will be ready to go when I get back from the AGA."

Janne nods her head but doesn't make eye contact, not that I expected her to.

"Thanks."

I shrug my shoulders and leave the odd girl to her puzzle. She might have a gift for details, but she doesn't have a gift for interacting with people.

When I walk down the steps of the hotel, I don't see the AGA store Trine mentioned until I look to my left. Just past the line of buses we drove in on is a small building with AGA – FRUKT, TOBAKK, SJOKOLADE in capital letters on its side. It also has a sign on the roof with a giant smoldering cigarette just behind the letters. I don't even read Norwegian and I can figure out what tobakk means.

Right inside the door is a round rack full of postcards. I pick out one that has a train on it with a mountain behind it, which kind of sums up most of my time in Norway so far. If the train was next to a river, it would be just perfect, but this one is good enough.

I'm about to pay for the postcard when I recognize some people I know out the window of the store. It's Georg and Inger. They're standing next to the same black car I saw them get into outside the Trondheim train station. They are both standing around a trash can peeling an orange as their driver is filling their car up with gas. I guess they changed their plans and decided to come to Bodø anyway.

My mouth starts to water as Inger pulls her orange apart and puts a whole section in her mouth. Then I remember the word FRUKT on the outside of the building, and I start looking around the store for the fruit. There are apples, oranges, bananas, and pears placed neatly in large, round baskets. I pick up an orange and put it to my nose. The last time I had an orange was on Christmas morning.

It's still amazes me how, in the middle of a Wisconsin winter, when there is two feet of snow on the ground and the wind whipping down from Canada drops the temperature to below zero, we can get that sweet orange fruit in our stocking. Peter and Max think an orange is about as desirable a gift as a new pair of underwear, so their oranges get left among the wrapping paper for me to find when I'm helping Mom clean up. I didn't understand how it even would be possible to get an orange in December until I pulled out our handy, dandy encyclopedia. If my brothers knew those oranges had traveled over a thousand miles (though before we grew them in the states, they came from Asia – even farther away), they might have a better appreciation for them. But the tart, orange smell also reminded me that this Christmas was the last one I would have with my dad. I put the orange down and take my postcards to the register.

When I exit the store, I turn toward the gas station to say hi to Georg and Inger, but before I can get close, they get in their car and speed out of the station like they're in a big hurry. Since they are heading away from me, they don't see me run up behind them.

I saw a piece of paper fall out of Georg's pocket as he got in the car, so I pick it up. I don't know if I will see them again, but you never know. They were so nice to me on the train, the least I can do is hold the paper for them in case it's important and our paths happen to cross again. Bodø isn't a big city like Oslo, so it's a lot more likely we'll meet again.

I unfold the paper and notice that it's a telegram. At the top is today's date and Georg's full name: Georg Christenson. But when I look at it a bit closer, it looks like something Danny, my five-year-old brother, would have done when we play school in our basement. Unlike Danny's writing, all the letters are legible, because they were typed out, but I can't even read Norwegian and I can tell these letters are all mixed up. It doesn't look like any Norwegian I've come across so far.

ILQQH IDJ VWRSSH IROJH DNWLYLWHW VWRSSH PDNWSDOLJJHQGH D ILQQH XW KYD GH YHW RP DPHULNDQVN PLGGHO VWRSSH LNNH PLVW HOOHU DQQHW VWRSSH

"That's odd. I should show this to Grandma," I say out loud, then fold it back up and put it in my shoulder-bag.

I walk down to the corner of what looks like the main street in town and look both directions but don't see their car anywhere. I'm really close to the water, so I decide I might as well walk a little farther and check it out. I cross the street and walk just half a block more to stand on the edge of the bay.

Where I'm standing is high up, away from the water. It's obviously a place where boats tie up. In fact, there's what looks like a fishing boat tied up about twenty yards to my left. A couple blocks farther I can see a really long pier where motorboats and sailboats are tied up in slips. That's also where the bay opens up to the ocean once it gets past the peninsula that's right across from me and the two large islands just behind that. Unfortunately, it means I can't dip my toe in anywhere close by. To my right, farther into the bay, the buildings turn to homes and the cement changes to rocks and grass.

The bay is about as wide as the Mississippi right next to De Soto, so I can easily see what looks like the foundation of an old building on the rocky peninsula straight across from me. *That must be the ruins Trine was talking about.*

I look at my wrist and remember (again) that I gave my watch to Yusuf. I turn and head back for the hotel. I don't want Grandma to worry about me, and I really want her opinion on Georg's telegram.

A

When I get back to the hotel, Trine is standing behind the desk and Janne is right behind her trying to tune in the radio. It screeches and whines until a song suddenly comes in loud and clear. Some young guys are singing a song about asking a postman if they brought them a letter. It's a catchy little tune, and I can't help but stop and listen along.

"My brother Adam would like that music," I say to Janne. "Who is that?"

She's standing next to the radio, nodding her head to the beat. Janne looks at me briefly, then turns back to the radio. "It's a group called The Beatles. They're a new group out of the United Kingdom. This is their first performance on Teenager's Turn – Here We Go."

"Teenager's Turn?"

Janne whips her head back to face me. "It's Teenager's Turn – Here We Go," she says in a tone that lets me know I didn't get it right. She immediately turns back to the radio, which I thought was the end of it, but boy was I wrong.

"It is a BBC radio program that airs every Saturday. They have all the latest groups on. The Beatles may be new, but I think they are wonderful.

The group is made up of four members: John Lennon, Paul McCartney, George Harrison, and Peter Best. They play clubs in England and Germany. Sometimes we can pick up stations from Germany. That's when I first heard them. They were a warm-up band for Tony Sheridan, but I like them much better than Mr. Sheridan; he has been around longer, of course, but..."

Trine interrupts her sister, who appeared to be just picking up steam. "Thanks, Janne," she says as she sets her hand softly on her sister's shoulder. "That is very interesting." Trine then turns to me as Janne walks around the counter and picks up her pencil and puzzle.

I stare at Janne in disbelief. A girl who has hardly said two words to us, wouldn't let my grandmother touch her to give her a tip, and won't look you straight in the eye, wasn't going to stop talking until her sister interrupted her. Now I'm really confused.

Trine gets my attention again by asking, "Did you find a postcard you liked, Miss Kelly?"

"Yeah, thanks. And you can call me Agnes."

I put my shoulder-bag on the counter, fish out the postcard, and hand it to Trine, then I find the telegram.

I lower my voice, even though it's only the three

of us in the room. With the odd things that have been happening to Grandma Agee and me: my dad dying under suspicious circumstances; the man with the ugly tiepin following us; and Colonel Wagner and Mr. Borge knowing things about us that we never told them, I don't want anyone overhearing. "I... found this by the AGA. I wonder if maybe you and your sister could help me figure out what it means. It fell out of the pocket of a man we met on the train on our trip here. I think it's in Norwegian, but I'm not sure."

I unfold the paper and hand it to her.

She looks it over a minute before she comes around to the front of the desk. "The letters look all mixed up."

"Exactly!"

"Let me show Janne. She's better at puzzles."

Janne looks up at the mention of her name then quickly back down.

Trine steps in front of her sister and puts the telegram on top of her crossword puzzle. "What do you think this is, Janne?"

Janne picks it up and not two seconds later, sets it on the chair beside her. "It's a substitution cipher." Then she goes back to working on her puzzle.

Janne's disinterest doesn't seem to faze Trine.

She picks up the telegram and sits down next to her sister. I sit down next to Trine.

"Can you help us decode it?" Trine asks.

Janne sets her folded newspaper down on the table and adjusts it so it is sitting just how she wants it. I didn't see it because of the newspaper, but she has a notepad in her hand which is about the size of the folded newspaper she was working on. She opens the cardboard cover and leafs through page after page of neatly written lists of word. I'm a little shocked to find out that this strange girl keeps word lists just like I do. I know I'm a bit strange, and not just because Adam tells me I'm strange. I don't fit in much with my classmates. I like words, especially Latin words, and I like looking up things. I like to read A LOT! Boys don't make me act silly like they seem to do for most of the girls in my class, and I don't let other girls bother me either. I think that's probably why Peggy is my only real close friend. She lives right next door, and we've known each other since we were babies. I'm not exaggerating either. Her birthday is two days before mine, so our moms were in the hospital at the same time. Peggy says we waved to each other from our bassinets at the hospital. I think she's crazy, but that's part of why I like her.

When Janne gets to a clean page in her notepad, she stops and takes the telegram from her sister without looking at her. I guess it's not just strangers Janne doesn't like to look at.

She starts by circling matching sets of letters.

I lean in so I can see what she's doing.

The sets of letters are all the same: VWRSSH. She writes those letters in her notebook. It takes her a few seconds but she starts to write the decoded word below the coded one.

"Stop!" I yell out before she is finished, then I cover my hand over my mouth.

Janne actually lifts her head and looks at me this time. So does Trine. I'm embarrassed by my outburst, but I couldn't help myself. I know what the answer is.

I know the answer because I have seen some old telegrams in a scrapbook my mom made from my dad's time in the service. Those telegrams used the same word at the end of each sentence like this one does. They had sent Grandma and Grandpa a telegram when he was wounded the first time. (My dad was wounded three different times — twice from what he called shrapnel [*n: small metal pieces that scatter outwards from an exploding bomb, shell, or mine*] and once when he twisted his ankle jumping out of a plane.) And Grandma Agee gave the telegram to my mom. I didn't know my mom made scrapbooks until I found it in our basement on a bookshelf. When I showed it to her, she said she had put it together before us kids were born, when she had more time.

Janne finishes decoding the word.

"But they spelled it wrong," I say. "It should be s-t-o-p."

Trine shakes her head. "In Norwegian it is spelled s-t-o-p-p-e. The message must be in Norwegian."

"That makes sense because this belongs to Georg, and..." I stop myself before I give too much away. "Yeah, that makes sense," I say instead.

"It is a Caesar cipher," Janne says.

"What's a Caesar cipher?" I ask.

"It is a cipher that Julius Caesar used when he wanted to keep his correspondence a secret. Which probably wasn't too hard since most of the people in his time period could not read, anyway. But this is a simple substitution cipher; it uses a shift of three letters. A is d, b is e, c is f, and so on. If they really wanted to keep this message secret, they should have used a Vigenère cipher. That is a very difficult cipher, indeed. It is a polyalphabetic substitution cipher that shifts the letters by different amounts using a key word or phrase known by both parties. I would have to create a Vigenère table to figure..."

Trine touches her sister's shoulder. "Yes, Janne, that is very interesting, but we need to decode this message." She directs Janne back to the telegram.

Janne looks back down at the paper and continues to work out the rest of the letters as if nothing happened.

From figuring out stoppe, Janne is able to put the decoded letters S, T, O, P, and E under the coded letters V, W, R, S, and H in the other words of the telegram. She also put a letter A under the coded letter D since that's the first letter in the alphabet.

ILQQH IDJ VWRSSH   IROJH   DNWLYL-
_ _ _ _E _A_ STOPPE _Ø_ _E _ _T_ _ _-

WHW VWRSSH
 T E T   STOPPE

PDNWSDOLJJHQGH D ILQQH XW KYD
_A _TPA_ _ _ _ _E_ _E A _ _ _ _E _T _ _A

GH YHW RP
_E _ET O_

DPHULNDQVN PLGGHO VWRSSH LNNH
A_E_ _ _ A_S_   _ _ _ _E_ STOPPE _ _ _E

PLVW HOOHU DQQHW VWRSSH
_ _ST E_ _ E_ A_ _ET STOPPE

Before I can think much more about it, she hands Trine her notebook.

FINNE FAG STOPPE FØLGE AKTIVITET
STOPPE MAKTPÅLIGGENDE Å FINNE UT
HVA DE VET OM AMERIKANSK MIDDEL
STOPPE IKKE MIST ELLER ANNET STOPPE

The only other word that I think I know, other than stop/stoppe is American/Amerikansk.

"Can you translate that for me?" I ask Trine.

Trine puts her hand on Janne's shoulder and slowly takes Janne's pencil (though she gives it up with some reluctance [n: *feeling or showing doubt about doing something*]), and writes the message in English just below the Norwegian.

Find subjects Stop Monitor activity Stop Imperative to find out what they know about American pilot Stop Do not lose again or else Stop

"Now I'm really confused. Georg and Inger said they were on vacation, but it sounds like they have been watching someone, actually more than one person, and the people they are following must have come to Bodø."

And who is the American pilot? Was it someone who works for Colonel Wagner or Mr. Borge? Someone my dad knew or maybe even someone he worked with?

"I better show this to my grandmother," I say, reaching for the notepad. "Something is rotten in the state of Denmark."

Janne's eyes get bigger the closer my hand gets to her notepad. Trine hands the notebook back to her sister.

Janne glances up at me, then back down to her notepad. "That's a quote from Shakespeare's play, Hamlet," Janne says without looking up. "Everyone thinks it was Hamlet that said those words, but it was Marcellus. He was talking to Horatio, though Hamlet was standing there as well. All three men were..."

"That is very interesting," Trine says and touches her sister again. Trine then turns to me. "I will get a piece of paper and copy it down for you."

That quote is something I hear my mom say when there is something that isn't quite right – from my brothers leaving food in their room way too long, to when money goes mysteriously missing from her purse. Now that I know she used to be an English teacher before us kids came along, it makes sense that she would be quoting Shakespeare.

Trine stands to go behind the desk again but I stop her.

"I've got paper," I say. I had forgotten about my composition notebook in my shoulder-bag.

I pull out the notebook and copy down the decrypted telegram. I put the telegram in the notebook, put my notebook back in my bag, and flip the lid closed.

Trine touches the pair of Pan Am wings that I got on my flight to New York. "I have a pair of wings just like these. An American pilot gave them to me. He was a very nice man. He said he had a daughter who was about my age, but she had red hair instead of blond hair."

Trine looks up at me and she suddenly looks like I have a booger sticking out of my nose.

She immediately gets up, goes to the counter, and pages through the ledger. Curious, I walk over to her and watch what she's doing. She finds what she's looking for, turns the book to face me, and puts her finger above a name with a capital letter A behind it.

I run my fingers over the name and my knees suddenly go weak. I have to lean on the counter so I don't fall down.

There, on the third line from the top, is the name Lt. Patrick D. Kelly.

Chapter Ten

I'm sitting in one of the lobby chairs, resting my arms on my thighs when Grandma Agee comes into the room.

"What in heaven's name..." she says as she sits down next to me.

I look up at her but don't know what to say.

"Are you all right, child? You look like you've seen a ghost."

Grandma doesn't realize she's not that far off the mark. Just fifteen minutes ago I was going to the store for a postcard to send to my family. Now I've come to find out that the nice Norwegian couple that I thought were my friends lied to me about what they were doing in Norway, and I'm staying in the very hotel that my father stayed in when he visited Bodø. And on top of all that, Georg and Inger are somehow involved with an American pilot. Could the pilot be a friend of my dad's and they came to Bodø to find him? Is he in danger now?

"Grandma, Trine knows dad!"

"What?" Grandma turns in Trine's direction.

"Well, she knew him." I stand and show Grandma the ledger on the counter and point to my dad's name. "He stayed at this very hotel."

"Many military people stay here," Trine explains. "I did not remember that his last name and your last name are the same until I saw Agnes' pin."

Grandma looks back at the Pan Am pin on my bag.

Then I remember what else Trine said. "How did you know my dad was an American pilot?"

"He wore an American uniform with wings on his chest. All the American pilots look like that."

Grandma and I look at each other.

"And there is something else...It's about Georg and Inger," I say, then pull out my notebook and open it to Georg's telegram.

I start to unfold the paper when one of the hotel doors opens. We all look at who just walked in. I turn back to my bag and immediately stuff the telegram and notebook back in my bag.

"Well, Mrs. Kelly…Agnes, I didn't think we'd meet up with you again!" Georg and Inger both come over and shake Grandma's hand. Georg puts his hand on my shoulder, and I have to try real hard not to move away; it feels like a fifty-pound weight holding me down, almost like he doesn't want me to move.

"After we were done sightseeing in Trondheim, we had a couple more days left of our vacation. We remembered that you were going to Bodø so we thought we'd come here too. But we never thought we'd meet up again."

Really? is all I can think. *That's not what the telegram said. I have to signal Trine somehow so she doesn't say something to Georg about the telegram.*

It takes me a minute, but after Georg asks Trine in Norwegian if they have any vacant rooms, I get an idea.

"Trine, is-thay elegram-tay elong-bay o-tay ese-thay eople-pay, ut-bay ey-thay ust-may ot-nay ow-knay I-yay ave-hay t-iay. I-yay on't-day ust-tray em-thay."

"Kay-oay," is Trine's reply, and I know the message was received.

Grandma Agee, Georg, and Inger are looking at me crosswise, but I do what any self-respecting kids does when they don't have a good answer for what just happened; I give them my most innocent smile. *Maybe this spy thing runs in the family,* I think with some satisfaction [n: the state of being satisfied or happy].

"So...any recommendations for sights?" Georg asks us as he pulls a Norwegian guidebook out of his pocket and starts to page through it.

My guidebook is for all of Scandinavia, so the section on Norway isn't real big, and it doesn't say anything about Bodø, I guess because the city is too small. We were going to go wherever Trine and Janne suggested.

"We rented a car in Trondheim, so we can go wherever we like," Georg says.

"We've had other business to tend to since we've been here, so today is our first chance to look around," Grandma Agee says.

This information seems to interest Georg by the bright look on his face. "Did you find Mr. Borge?"

It takes Grandma a minute before she speaks. And much to my relief "We did" is all Grandma says.

When she doesn't share anything more, Inger

adds to the conversation. "I hope he was able to help you."

"Not as much as we had hoped."

Grandma puts her arm around my shoulder and gives it a squeeze. That's when I notice the distinct smell of tobacco on her clothes. I thought grandma was in our room writing a letter. She must have gone someplace else, someplace where people were smoking.

"Well, how about we see the sights together," Inger suggests. "We've got a nice big car."

"Trine and Janne were going to show us around," I say quickly, "but thank you for the offer."

Now that I know Trine and Janne have both met my dad, I don't want to lose the opportunity to pick their brains about what they know about his time in Bodø. I'd love to be able to bring back at least a little information about my dad since Grandma and I can't tell my family the really important news: that he wasn't an insurance salesman but really worked for the CIA; that he was in Bodø, Norway before he died, not Turkey, like the government told us; and, by the way, he is a spy. Besides, Georg and Inger are lying through their teeth, I can just tell, so going with them is out of the question.

("Pick their brains" is a great idiom, don't you

think? I can just imagine a door in someone's head as I look in and pick out thoughts and words with a very small tweezers. Isn't that deliciously disgusting?)

"I think that would be very nice," Grandma Agee says.

My eyes go wide and my body tightens. *No, Grandma! We can't go with these people! They lied to us. They can't be trusted!*

"We would be happy to be your guides," Trine says, though her sister doesn't look like she likes the idea any more than I do.

Well, now we're painted into a corner. It's not too hard to figure out what that idiom means. If Grandma wants to go with them and Trine wants to go with them, I don't see any way around it; we're stuck going.

Georg hesitates, like he's not sure about the plan either, but then agrees. "It'll be a tight fit, but if Agnes is willing to sit in the front with Inger and myself, we will manage."

Trine goes to tell her mother where we are going, and soon we are outside the hotel looking at the same big, black car I saw in the gas station next to the AGA store. I look inside and the driver is nowhere to be seen.

Did they tie him up and put him in the trunk? I wonder.

When they open the car door, the sweet smell of orange comes wafting [*v: to move lightly through the air*] out and my stomach turns upside down. We all get in, me in the front between Inger and Georg; and Grandma, Trine, and Janne in the back.

I don't know about you, but when I am nervous, I sing to myself. I can't sing out loud at the moment so I sing in my head the first song that comes to me:

On top of spaghetti, all covered with cheese,
I lost my poor meatball, when somebody sneezed.

I hold my bag tight to my chest as Inger reaches down to get the bag at her feet.

It rolled off the table, and onto the floor, and
then my poor meatball, rolled right out the door.

I wonder what she's going to take out of her bag: a rope to tie us up or maybe a gun so they can demand we take them to find the pilot they're looking for. I start humming to myself.

It rolled into the garden, and under a bush,
and then my poor meatball, is nothing but mush.

She reaches in her bag and pulls out...an orange!

Yup, an orange!

"We bought these delicious oranges at the store this morning. Would you like to share it with your grandmother and your friends?" Inger says, all sweetness and smiles.

My mouth starts to water at the prospect, but I know how expensive that orange was, so I politely turn down the offer. Maybe I have Georg and Inger all wrong. Maybe they aren't the bad people I think they are. They did give me that map and spent all that time on the train telling us about the countryside.

Georg turns to the back. "Where to first?"

No one says anything right away, so I speak up. "I'd like to put my feet in the ocean before we leave," I say.

"Then you will want to visit the Nyholms Skandse bastion," Janne says. "It is on the island across the bay. In this way you will be able to step in the ocean and visit a historic Norwegian tourist destination at the same stop. It is more efficient that way and since you only have one day before you have to leave, it is..."

"Janne," Trine says and touches her sister's knee, redirecting her before her sister can continue on whatever tangent she was about to embark on.

"Can you tell everyone about the bastion, the fort?" [To go off on a tangent means *to start talking about something that is only slightly or indirectly related to the original subject.* A tangent is actually a geometry term: *a line that touches a circle or sphere at only one point.*] And without skipping a beat, Janne starts in about the how the fort was built in 1810 during the Napoleonic war to keep the English from invading Hundholman, which is what Bodø was called way back then. She said there was an important fish factory and grain storage bins in town that they wanted to protect. Then Janne starts to veer off again, talking about the current fishing industry in Bodø and in all of Norway since it's such a big part of their country's economy. She tells us that Norway is the fifth largest fish producer in the world. That makes sense, of course, since three-quarters of the country's border is along the ocean, and according to my travel guide, has some of the warmest water because of the Gulf Stream that goes right by Norway.

It takes us less than fifteen minutes to get to the end of the peninsula – though Janne said it used to be an island – where we park along a narrow road that leads up to what used to be the stone walls of the fort. When we get out of the car, I notice two boxy-looking, white houses, one two-stories tall, the other, just one, that sit off to the left. I don't know if they cut down all the trees or if they didn't have enough soil to grow in but there is nothing on the entire island but scrub brush and tall grass clinging in patches to the rough, gray rock.

We walk up toward the piles of stones and dirt at the peak of the rock formation with Janne and Trine in the lead. Inger has Grandma Agee's arm, and Georg hangs back to walk with me. It's a lovely day with a few thin, white clouds high in the otherwise robin's egg-blue sky. A soft, cool breeze off the water plays with my hair, sending it this way and that and keeps any bugs from landing.

"How was your train ride from Trondheim?" Georg asks.

I have to squint into the bright sky to look up at him; he seems taller now that I'm standing right next to him. "It was really nice, like you said it would be. The sound of the wheels on the tracks and the sway of the train car put me right to sleep."

"That happens to me every time," he says with a smile.

"But I think I could have slept through anything. We weren't able to sleep in a real bed during our trip from Turkey."

"How awful."

We walk along a dirt path on the city side of the old fort, making our way toward an opening in the piles of rock.

"Who did you visit with in Turkey?" Georg hesitates, then continues on. "I remember you said someone there told you about Mr. Borge."

"You have a good memory, Georg. Yeah, my dad's partner in Turkey told Grandma Agee about Mr. Borge."

"Was your father's partner a pilot too?"

I stop walking and look at Georg. "I...don't actually know," I say, then start walking again. "I don't remember my grandma telling you my dad was a pilot."

"Oh, you must have," he says as easy as pie. "I couldn't have made that up."

Of course, *easy as pie* is another idiom. Making pie isn't easy, but eating one is, that is if you like pie, and I *like* pie!

There is an opening in the mounds of dirt and stones and the ground inclines further as we make our way inside the collapsed walls. *Georg has to be right*, I think, *Grandma must have said something about dad being a pilot. But I don't usually forget things like that. I guess I've been more distracted since I've been traveling, so I don't remember things like I do when I'm at home.* Looking straight out at what looks like hardly a stone's-throw away, is another big rock island. This one has very little grass and no shrubs at all. It's also much longer than the rock island we're standing on.

Without being asked, Janne picks up with her tour guide duties. "That island has the name of Litle Hjartøya (*lit-la yar-toe-ya*). The larger island behind it that you cannot see has the name of Store Hjartøya (*stew-rea yar-toe-ya*). Litle Hjartoya has no inhabitants, but Store is large enough to be occupied on the leeward side, though it is only accessible by boat."

I look to my left, back at Bodø, and there are three large mountaintops along the coastline to the south, all of which have snow on their peaks. When I face the city, I also see multiple mountain peaks that appear as if they are just behind the buildings, a formidable [*adj: large or impressive in size or amount*] wall of impassible stone, though I know that's not the case because Grandma and I passed among them ourselves just yesterday. Man, that seems like a long time ago. It almost looks like the mountains are out of place behind a very modern city scene, but I know it should be the other way around. The mountains were here long before the people showed up.

Looking to the north, the hills are not as tall, and I can tell they are covered by trees because of the dark-green color that coats them all like a fuzzy blanket.

I turn back to face Litle Hjartoya, and I notice that the rock wall of the old fort drops straight down to a small, flat area. There are two buildings painted dark-red that are a bit bigger than the white ones we saw when we got out of the car, though they are built in the same simple, boxy style. There is a docking area all along the water's edge next to the buildings so I suspect the red buildings have something to do with the fishing boats we passed on our way along the peninsula.

"During WWII the Germans set up artillery and built a bunker in the bastion as they did throughout the city," Janne explains.

I look around for the best place to put my feet into the water, and it looks like the southern tip of the island might fit the bill. "Is that a light?" I ask Janne as I point to the south. There is a short, white, round object with a red roof that looks like a miniature lighthouse perched at the south edge of the rock. I can see the same thing on the southern tip of Litle Hjartøya as well. I imagine these rocks are pretty hard to see in the dark, especially if there is a strong storm and the sea is very rough.

"Yes, it helps the boats avoid hitting the island."

"Do you think I can put my feet in the water there? It looks like it's more of a gradual drop to the water than around most of the rest of the peninsula."

"Yes, that would be an ideal location," Janne says.

I immediately exit the old fortification and run along a one-person path toward the water's edge. It feels good to stretch my legs. I haven't had a good run in a very long time.

I hear Grandma Agee's voice in the distance. "Wait, Agnes!"

And moments later Georg has jogged up to join me.

"Your Grandmother was worried about you, so I said I'd make sure you were okay. I'm a strong swimmer, and I know first-aid."

"Me too," I say. "I live right next to the Mississippi River so my parents made sure all us kids could swim. And I used to be a Girl Scout, until the scout leader got tired of me telling her how to do things. So I know basic first aid."

"Ha! Why does that not surprise me," he says with a chuckle.

I get to the water's edge, take my bag off my

shoulder, sit down on the rock, and start to undo my saddle shoes. I put on slacks this morning in anticipation of roaming the city (Grandma agreed with slacks but wouldn't let me wear my jeans), so I have to roll up my pant legs to keep them dry. Georg is a gentleman and helps me to standing, and I gingerly make my way to the water. It's early in my summer vacation and my feet haven't been out of shoes much this year, so it's a bit slower going than it would be if I'd had all summer to toughen them up. I looked back at Grandma, who is sitting on a small stone wall about forty feet away, along with Inger and Janne. Trine is walking toward Georg and me.

"Be careful. The rocks may be slippery," Georg warns.

I have slipped on many a slimy rock in the Mississippi, so I know what to look out for. Luckily the water is crystal clear and I can easily see where I'm going.

Trine catches up with us just as I dip a few toes in to see if I can go in all the way. I know it's supposed to be warmed from the Gulf Stream, but we're at the same latitude as Alaska, so I know it won't be bathwater-warm like the river at home can get on a hot August day.

"It will be a bit cold, but I will swim in it if it's a very hot day," Trine says.

I can't help but squeal as I put both feet all the way under. A shiver runs up my spine and my body shakes for just a second as if to tell me this isn't such a good idea. I ignore this primal instinct and step out a little farther. Trine smiles as my ankles go under, my toes now quickly acclimated [*v: to adjust or adapt to a new climate, place, or situation*] to the cold.

"I must return to Janne, Miss Agnes. She does not like the water, so we will meet you back at the bastion."

"Oh, all right," I say. "Trine, your sister is very lucky to have you."

"I know she is a little...different, but she is my sister."

I nod my head in understanding. "I won't be long," I say as she turns to leave.

As annoying as my brothers can be sometimes, they do have some good qualities. And I would miss them if they were gone.

"That looks like fun. Do you mind if I join you?" Georg sits down on the rocks and proceeds to take his shoes and socks off as well.

"No, of course not," I say, though if I was being truthful, I'd really rather he just stay on shore. He and Inger haven't done anything weird since they found us this morning, but that telegram still makes me wary. The sooner we get this sightseeing trip over with the better, as far as I'm concerned.

A small fishing boat goes close by the tip of the peninsula as Georg steps into the water. A bearded man in overalls, a flannel shirt, and a stocking cap waves as they chug leisurely by. I smile and wave back. I look back at Grandma, who waves and smiles at the fisherman too. I can see Janne and Trine walk, one behind the other, back to the old fort. I step farther out so the water rises up to the middle of my calves, a new level of cold gripping tightly around my legs.

"Did you find out anything about your father from Mr. Borge?"

I decide to be honest with Georg in hopes that it ends his questions. "Nothing I can tell you about." If I can't tell my family what we found out about my dad, I'm certainly not going to tell a Georg.

Georg laughs. "Is it a state secret?"

Now he's making me more uncomfortable again. I don't know why he's so interested in what Mr. Borge told us. He had asked Grandma the same thing. I suppose he thinks because I'm a dumb kid and my grandma isn't standing here, I'll spill the beans.

"Something like that," is all I say as I watch the way the rippling water makes my feet look like a Picasso painting, toes going this way and that.

"That is most unfortunate...because you really will need to tell me."

I look up from watching the water and stare at him. Georg's Norwegian accent just changed to something quite different. "What did you say?"

Then I remember what Grandma said on the train – or what she *didn't* say! She didn't tell Georg or Inger Mr. Borge's name, and come to think about it, she never said anything about my dad's partner in Turkey being a pilot, I'm sure of it!

But it's too late. Georg steps a little closer, then waves at Inger, who waves back. Then he turns, graps tightly to my arm, and stares back at me. Actually, he's glaring at me, which if you look it up, means *to stare angrily or fiercely.* "I said you need to tell me what Mr. Borge told you." Then quick as a snake he turns me to face the shore. "Because Inger will harm your grandmother if you do not," he says through clenched teeth.

Suddenly I don't feel the cold anymore; all I can see is Grandma Agee looking at me. Inger is now standing behind my grandmother, holding what appears to be a gun in her raised arm. Grandma must not see her because she smiles and waves like it's just another day at the beach.

"Smile and wave back," Georg says, giving my arm an un-needed squeeze.

I raise my arm and give a small wave but I can't manage much of a smile.

"There, that wasn't so hard," he whispers in my ear. "Your papa will be so proud of you."

Amazingly, I'm not afraid. My heart is racing, I can feel it pounding in my chest, but I'm not afraid. All I can think about is my grandmother innocently watching me take my first dip in the ocean as her life hangs in the balance. Now that's one idiom I suddenly fully understand.

Do I tell this stranger something that we were sworn not to tell, something that could put the United States at risk, something that could be the very thing that killed my own father, or do I push him in the water and run like my life depends on it, or to be more accurate, like my grandma's life depends on it? At a good forty yards away, I doubt I could get to Grandma Agee before Inger decided to harm her. And what could I do, anyway? I could try and hit Inger with my shoulder-bag, but would that work?

I stop thinking, turn to Georg, and with all my

strength, push him over. He doesn't expect it so he falls right in with a splash. I sprint out of water, grabbing my shoulder-bag on my way out. I swing it over my head as I run toward Inger and my grandmother. It takes Inger a moment but eventually she pulls Grandma Agee to standing and shoves the gun in her back. I make it up to them in less than a minute, and I circle around them both, swinging my bag over and over above my head in a large arch, waiting for the right moment to strike as Inger keeps Grandma Agee between her and me.

All right. Yes, I'm imagining things again. I was just running it through my mind to see if it might work. What I don't anticipate is that Georg has a gun too. He's just pulled it out from his jacket pocket, and he's got it poking in my back, for real. Now *I am* afraid, and I have to try real hard not to pee my pants. I reach up and grasp Dad's Saint Christopher metal and Yusuf's evil eye pendent. If I had needed help with anything in my life, I need it now.

"Time is up, Agnes. You no longer have a choice. Tell me what I want to know."

All I can think is what I heard both my grandma and Dad say: *You always have a choice.*

Before I have a chance to do or say anything, I hear a man call my name, then two words I would have never expected in my wildest dreams: "Op-dray ow-nay!"

And without thinking, I jab Georg in the stomach as hard as I can with my elbow, and I dive for the icy-blue water.

Chapter Eleven

As I go down, I see my grandmother stand and swing her purse around behind her. I don't get to see if she makes contact with what or, more accurately, who she's swinging at because there is something flying over top of me and blotting out the sun.

When I come up for air, there is a man who looks like he just stepped out of The Aquanauts TV program. He is wearing a black rubber diving suit, scuba mask, and matching black fins as he handcuffs Georg's arms behind his back. There are two other men, both in a similar get-up, running up to my grandmother, who is sitting on something, no, *someone* on the ground, though they have lost their fins and are running in just their bare feet. When

I get up on my knees, I can see Janne and Trine running for my grandmother, as well.

"Are you all right, Agnes?"

I flip the wet hair off of my face and turn to the diver kneeling next to Georg. Georg must be knocked out because he is still face down on the rock, not moving. I don't see any blood, so I don't think he's dead, which is a good thing. I've seen lots of dead animals because my dad was a hunter: deer, squirrels, rabbits...but seeing a dead person would be something else entirely.

The man has his mask off now and is in the process of peeling off his rubber headpiece. And who appears underneath the black rubber suit but the man with the steel-blue eyes. I sit back in the water, completely oblivious to the cold that surrounds me.

A

I'm sitting with a blanket around my shoulders next to my grandmother in the biggest of the two white-washed houses we first saw when we stepped out of the car. It obviously used to be someone's home, from the kitchen I spied when they brought us in, but there isn't a stick of furniture in sight, other than the chairs the local police have brought in for us to sit on while we give our statements to the US CIA officers. One of those officers is the man with the steel-blue eyes, who we now know as Officer Miller. He is wearing a flannel shirt and overalls like the man on the fishing boat, but Officer Miller doesn't have a beard (at least not now). He's sitting opposite us with a secretarial type notepad like Janne had and a pen. I have a million questions running through my head, most notably, who really are Georg and Inger, and why were they so interested in what we knew about what happened to my father? I had already figured out that Grandma and I were the people they were following. That's obvious, now, but the question is why?

The police are standing guard inside and outside the building along with Norwegian troops from the air base in town. There was also a small crowd from the industrial buildings along the peninsula and even a few people across the bay looking on as they led Georg and Inger away in handcuffs to waiting cars, escorted by the local police, red lights flashing as they drove off the island.

They have placed Grandma and me in one room and Janne and Trine in another. They wanted to interview me by myself, but Grandma insisted that we stay together. If they didn't want to honor that request, "we'll both keep our gobs shut and you wouldn't learn a darn thing" as Grandma had put it.

As it is, I don't think they're learning much from us, anyway. They were very interested in the telegram I showed them, however, whisking it away after Officer Miller had copied it down in his notepad. I explained how I found it and how Trine and Janne had helped me decode it.

"Janne could tell right away it was a Caesar cypher, so it didn't take her long to decode."

"How did she know it was a Caesar cypher?" Officer Miller asks.

"I don't know. Even though she acts a little odd, she seems to know a lot about a lot of things."

A small smile spreads across the officer's face. "I've noticed," he says.

"And you hadn't met the Iversen sisters before your arrival yesterday at..." He flips through his notepad to find what he's looking for. "Eleven thirty, June 21."

"Of course not," my grandmother says, obvious annoyance [n: *to be disturbed or irritated*] in her voice. "They're innocent children. They were just trying te help us. I hope you aren't givin' them the third degree like you're doin' te us. They must be frightened half out of their wits, the poor dears."

I think Grandma is getting tired of the endless

questions. I notice they have asked us to verify [*v: to prove or check the truth, accuracy, or reality of*] certain bits of information at least two different times, making sure to ask the same question in a different way each time, as if they were trying to catch us in a lie. Grandma must have noticed it too.

"Will you be able to tell who sent Georg and Inger the telegram, if that is even their real names," I say.

Officer Miller doesn't look up from his notepad. "We're working on it," is all he says.

Grandma and I have both asked a few different questions about Georg and Inger, but he has dodged them each and every time. Maybe I need to push the point with a little information of my own, but Grandma beats me to the point.

"Listen, Mr. Miller," Grandma says.

"Officer Miller," he corrects her.

"Officer Miller. We've told you repeatedly, we didn't know the couple before they started talking to us on the train. They were very nice to Agnes, so I bought them dinner, that is all. I told them why we were here, just like I told you and the colonel at the air base..."

She then puts an arm around my shoulder and gives it a squeeze. "Agnes has been through a lot, as have I," she says.

I look down at her leg that now has a large bandage along her right shin, and her left elbow that is similarly covered, and I marvel at what my grandmother did to that young lady, whatever her name is.

A

Before Officer Miller came in to speak to us, I had asked Grandma how she managed to get the upper hand.

"I was a player on the winnin' Dublin camogie (*cae-mo-gea*) team in the all-Ireland championship in 1923. I was pretty good at wackin' a ball with a stick, so hitting Miss Inger, or whatever the girl's name is, with my purse was a piece a cake."

"Camogie?"

"It's kinda like hurlin', but it's just for women."

"I don't know what hurling is either," I said.

"You play football in the States, right?"

"Of course we do. Remember watching Peter and Max throwing the ball in the back yard?"

"Oh, yeah...actually, the football I'm referrin' to is what you all call soccer. Camogie is kind a like soccer but with a ball about the size of a baseball, and it's played with sticks that have a wide, flat end.

"We tussled a bit once I got 'er on the ground, but weight and determination will win out every time."

"How did you know what was going on?"

"I-ay ow-knay Ig-pay atin-lay oo-tay," she said with a smile.

"So you knew what I said to Trine!" I said with amazement. "Then why did you agree to go with them?"

"There is an old saying: Keep your friends close but your enemies closer. If there was somethin' amiss with those two and they wanted us to go with 'em, then we'd go with them."

I leaned into her, glad I had such an amazing granny.

A

"We've come a long way and been through an awful lot," Grandma says. "Been spied on..." Officer Miller looks down at this remark. "Been held, beaten, and had our very lives threatened. I think we deserve a few answers ourselves."

I sit up straight, nodding my head in agreement. *Go, Grandma, go! Fortes est veritas!* – Truth is strong!

Officer Miller closes his notepad, then looks at the door to make sure it's still closed.

He puts his forearms on his thighs, letting out a deep sigh. "Georg and Inger are known Russian spies." He says this like he's reading off the Sunday newspaper.

Both Grandma and I are bowled over. Of course, we don't tip over or anything, though I don't think it would have taken much to do that. We are both stunned into a petrified state [petrified – *adj: converted into stone, to be lifeless or inactive*]. It takes a minute for us even to blink.

"Mr. Borge has been monitoring their activity, but when they left you in Trondheim, we thought they had gotten the information they had wanted from you."

"So that *was* you on the train...just before we went into that tunnel," I say.

Officer Miller nods.

"Did you get off the train in Dombås?"

He smiles and sits up straight. "You had outed me again, Agnes, just like you did in the airplane, so I had no choice. I had an agent followed you to Bodø."

I think back to the train trip from Trondheim to Fauske. I don't remember seeing anyone watching us...though there was that lady train steward that helped us set up our bed and checked on us before we got to the station. Could it have been her? A lady CIA agent?!

"How did you know Georg and Inger had come to Bodø?" my grandmother asks.

"We didn't, until we heard their voices."

Grandma and I both look at each other, confused.

Officer Miller picks up my shoulder-bag from beside me and unpins the Pan Am wings from the front flap. He turns it over to reveal a small device glued to the back.

"Well I'll be a monkey's uncle," I say. I can't help but smile at the small, clever listening device.

"We didn't think they would contact you again, but we wanted to be sure."

"So that's how you knew I knew pig Latin."

He nods again.

"Is that something they teach you in spy school?" I ask.

"Believe it or not, Agnes, I was young once too."

Grandma puts her hands on her thighs and lets out a sigh. "Well, we appreciate your honesty, Officer Miller, and just like the information you and Mr. Borge shared with us at the air base, you can be sure what you've told us won't go outside this room. Will it, Agnes?"

I quickly agree. "Not a peep."

"I'm happy to hear it, ladies. These are perilous times, as you both well know. The Cold War is a serious thing," he says as he stands. He turns and walks toward the door.

Grandma and I stand too. "Officer Miller," I say. "I've got one more question for you."

He turns back around to face us. "When Georg was asking about my father, he knew my dad was a pilot. How did he know that?"

Officer Miller blinks his eyes rapidly and purses his lips before he finally speaks. "I would suspect they know a lot about our agents, just like we know a lot about them."

"But he talked about him in the present tense, like Mr. Borge did at the air base. Georg said my papa will be so proud of me."

Grandma sits slowly back down, staring at me but mostly staring through me. "Mr. Borge did do that, didn't he?" she says as she stares off into space, like she's looking at something in the distance. "And Mr. Brooks...in Turkey..." It takes Grandma a few seconds but she finally continues. "He said that 'Patrick *is* a patriot' not that Patrick *was* a patriot!"

We both turn to each other, then at the same time turn back to Officer Miller, who has turned a pasty white, like a black cat has just walked over his grave. He rubs a hand over his mouth, walks over to the door, and locks it.

When he turns back toward us, he looks like a man who is about to take some medicine he knows is going to taste really bad. "You both better sit down."

Chapter Twelve

I don't exactly know where the saying came from about the black cat walking over someone's grave because if you were actually in a grave, it wouldn't matter to you who or what walked over top of you. But it is a thing people say, and it seemed to describe the look on Officer Miller's face when he realized he had to tell us what was really going on, black cats being associated [*v: to happen together or are related or connected in some way*] with scary things, and all.

I am fanning Grandma Agee with my composition notebook as I help guide a glass of water to her mouth. She is slowly getting the color back into her cheeks as she takes smalls sips of the water. I'm as shocked as she is, but I don't know if it's because of what we have just gone through a couple hours ago or because I thought my grandma was going to pass out at the news, that I don't feel faint myself.

It's probably more that I really don't believe it yet, believe that my father is alive and well in a Russian prison or at least as well as a person can be in prison.

After a few minutes, Grandma calms down and starts to ask more questions.

"So why in God's name did ya tell us that he was dead?!"

Officer Miller takes in a deep breath and lets it out very slowly, as if he is giving himself time to come up with an answer.

"Because, Mrs. Kelly, no one is supposed to know what he was doing."

He stands up, goes behind his chair, and places his hands on the back, leaning on the chair for support.

"We weren't lying when we said this is a matter of national security. Only those working with your son and those in the highest positions within the CIA and the White House know what is going on, and now you will too."

Officer Miller has our undivided attention as he starts to pace back and forth in front of us. "Officer

Kelly has been working on a covert operation for over five years now. His history in the Air force as a WWII pilot was paramount for this work, plus he has exceptional ratings as a pilot, innumerable flight hours, top secret clearance, and he was a reserve officer so the Air Force could call him up at any time."

"What operation?" Grandma Agee asks.

The officer doesn't hesitate anymore; he's spilling beans all over the room. "Since the end of WWII and the beginning of the Cold War, we had no way to know what the Russians were doing: how close they were to launching a nuclear bomb, how many aircraft they had, or even how many intercontinental ballistic missiles were operational and where they had them, so Patrick and other pilots like him were hired and trained by the CIA to fly missions over Russia, taking pictures of their military installations and missile sites."

Grandma and I are stunned into silence once more. All I can think is *But how?!* Any plane I see in the sky is so high and going so fast, I can't imagine any picture they took would be anything but a blur. And now having been in a plane myself, once we got up to what they called a "cruising altitude," I could see lakes and rivers and large hills, but everything was too small to make out any details.

The looks on our faces must have given him a clue as to what we were thinking because he goes on to explain further.

"The Air Force developed a plane unlike anything it has had in the past. Commercial aircraft fly at approximately 30,000 feet. This plane, called the U2, can fly 60,000 to 70,000 feet above the earth, high enough that any normal plane would be unable to intercept it."

"Like a Soviet fighter," Grandma says.

Officer Miller nods his head slowly, with a look of surprise on his face. "Yes, exactly." I don't think he was expecting Grandma Agee to get the right answer. I wasn't either.

Then I remember the odd looking plane with the really long wings at the air base. "Is there a U2 plane at the air base in Bodø?" I ask.

Officer Miller looks at me like he thinks I'm psychic [*adj: sensitive to influences or forces believed to come from beyond the natural world*], like I could read his mind or something. "How did you know that?"

"Is it kind of small, with really long, thin wings?" He nods again.

"I saw it at the air base, in a hanger."

"Not much gets by you, does it, Agnes? We could use more people like you in the agency," he says with a smile. "The plane carries sophisticated cameras that are able to take pictures so clear you can make out the top of a manhole in the street."

I let out a long whistle.

"So what happened with my son?"

"We don't exactly know, Mrs. Kelly. When he didn't show up at his designated destination, we didn't know where he was in Russia or even if he was alive. After some false information from the Kremlin, we now know the Soviets have him in Vladimir Prison, east of Moscow, and they have his plane. They tell us he's in good shape, but we don't know about the plane."

"I don't care about your darn plane, Officer Miller; all I care about is my son. What are you doing to get him released?"

Now Officer Miller starts to squirm, like someone put itching powder down the back of his shirt. "Well...that's the other reason why we told you that he had died." He finally looks Grandma Agee in the eyes. "We don't think we can get him out."

All of a sudden, I can't catch my breath. It's like someone has punched me hard in the stomach and I can't breathe. All in a matter of one day, my father has gone from being dead to being alive. And now he's all but dead to us again, unable to get out of the Russian prison that's holding him.

Grandma sees my distress and now she helps me drink the water in the glass she's holding. The cool water seems to calm the fire in my belly, and Grandma's firm hand on my back helps me remember I'm not here going through this alone, which, even though it doesn't change what's happening, somehow makes the bad news a small bit easier to take.

"The Russians want to use him as an example: put him on trial for espionage and keep him incarcerated so that we don't attempt any more overflights. As long as they have him, they have us over a barrel."

Having someone over a barrel is another idiom, of course, since they aren't physically holding anyone in the CIA over a barrel other than maybe my father. If a person is "over a barrel," it means something is out of their control. I looked it up later and the saying – first written down in 1938 – is supposed to be from when they put a person who had drowned, over a barrel, head down, and rolled them back and forth to try and get the water out of their lungs. That must have been before they knew the modern technique for resuscitation that I learned in Girl Scouts.

"So what happens now?"

Officer Miller sits back down and leans his arms back on his thighs. "You and Agnes fly back home as planned, and we keep working to get your son out."

"What does working to get him out mean, exactly?" Grandma asks.

"Besides the diplomats, we have been talking to the Russian government..." He looks around the room as if somehow someone else snuck in while we weren't watching and is listening in on our conversation. Then he continues, lowering his voice. "We have a couple agents on the ground, checking out other options. They are a married couple who work in the prison, so they are able to get us some good intel – intelligence information – about your son's present situation. It's just that we can't rush things. Getting the information is one thing; getting your son out of the country without compromising the illegals or their handler is quite another."

"Illegals? Handler?" I say. All this CIA mumbo jumbo is confusing me.

"An illegal is an agent operating in a foreign country without diplomatic papers. A handler is the person who manages the agent, passes information to them and takes intel from them. As you can imagine, it's very risky for all of them. They're working under false papers, false identification, so if they are caught, they don't have any US government protection, unlike Lt. Kelly, who, according to the story we have given the Russians, was an Air Force officer on a weather reconnaissance flight out of Turkey when he accidentally drifted into Russian air space."

"So he *had* been in Turkey?" I say.

"Yes, most of the U2 flights have been out of Adana, Turkey, but not this flight. He actually flew out of Peshawar, Pakistan. He was scheduled to fly here, to Bodø, and when he didn't show when he was supposed to, we knew something went wrong."

"I wondered how Bodø fit in with all this," I say.

Grandma looks over at me and sighs, like she's not sure she wants to hear the answer to her next question. "So how will we know if you're successful?"

The officer sits back in his chair. "Because of the sensitive nature of this operation, you won't know until your son is released. We can't risk any messages getting intercepted. They'll be watching you and your family even closer now that their operatives in Norway have been captured."

They've been watching my family?! I wonder if they're watching Peggy too? I swallow hard at the thought.

"Even though I've shared this information with

you, it doesn't change the fact that you can't tell anyone else. You understand that anything that compromises this mission puts Patrick's life at risk." Officer Miller was looking at Grandma while he was talking, but now he turns his gaze to me. "You understand, Agnes. You can't tell anyone."

I make a large X over my heart. If he knows pig Latin, then he's got to know what that means.

Grandma reaches over and squeezes my hand. "We understand, Officer Miller."

The officer stands and unlocks the door. "We'll have a driver take you and the Iversen girls back to your hotel. It's late. I imagine you're all pretty hungry after all you've been through."

I hadn't noticed, but when I look outside, the sky is a dull gray.

"Officer Miller, I've got one more question for you." The officer stops and looks at me. "When you fell, or pretended to fall in the airplane, the one going to Paris, how did you know that I had a letter in my hand?"

The officer shakes his head and smiles before he answers. "How did you know I knew it was a letter?"

"You called it a letter even before you picked it up off the floor."

He put a finger up to his mouth as he thought

about what I had said. "You know, Agnes, I think you're right. I did give myself away, didn't I?"

I couldn't help but smile. I had been right! "Why did you trip or pretend to trip, I mean?"

"We wanted to know what was in that letter. We knew it was a letter from your father, and we knew you were going to Norway, but we didn't know why. We thought your father's letter might give us a clue."

"How did you know it was from my dad?"

He gives me a sly look. "I can't give away all our tricks, Agnes."

"But you didn't have time to read it," I say.

"I didn't need to read it, I just needed to hold it long enough to take a picture."

"A picture?!" my grandma and I say at the same time.

I beat Grandma to the next logical questions. "How did you take a picture?"

"My tiepin was a camera lens. All I have to do is squeeze the knot in my tie and I'm able to take a picture of whatever I am holding."

"I should have known that tiepin was ugly for a reason, but I'd have never guessed it was a camera!"

Officer Miller laughs. "I'll tell my wife that. She thinks it's ugly too."

Grandma walks up to Officer Miller and reaches

up to touch his face. He leans down to meet her half way. "Thank you for watching over us and protecting Agnes," Grandma says in a soft voice. Then she gets up on her tiptoes and kisses the officer's cheek.

I wouldn't have believed it if I hadn't seen it, but the officer blushes. "Thank you for helping us capture a couple of known Russian spies. We've been trying to get something on these two for years."

He turns to me and says, "And Agnes, keep studying hard. I wasn't joking when I said you'd make a great officer one day. Ave-hay a-yay ood-gay ight- flay," he says, then gives me a wink and he's gone. He's good at that, disappearing in a matter of seconds. I'll have to work on that if I'm really going to be a spy like my dad when I grow up.

Chapter Thirteen

Outside the Bodø airport there is a post that has signs pointing to various destinations. Each sign says how long it will take to fly to that city: London and the North Pole are only three hours away, four hours back to Paris, and twenty-one to Tokyo. But if you go over the North Pole, it would take only fourteen. It's supposed to take ten hours and fifteen minutes to get to New York City, then we have another four hours or so to get to Chicago, where we'll have to wait for Mom to come and pick us up. The long trip to Chicago will give Grandma and me plenty of time to come up with a good story to tell Mom and my brothers. I hope they believe us. I don't want to put my dad's life in any more danger than it already is.

We're standing at the check-in counter at the Bodø airport, this time on the commercial side of the runway. Grandma is getting our boarding passes, but I'm looking out the window, across the runway as a US military plane speeds by, tips its nose skyward, and is gone in a flash with only the roar of its engine in its wake [*n: a track or path left by a moving body*]. It's hard to imagine my dad flying one of those planes, but he probably did, and he even flew that strange looking U2 plane 60 or 70,000 feet in the sky.

I look up and try and imagine seeing a little black speck flying overhead. But it wouldn't be my dad in that speck; my dad is sitting in a Russian prison, and we don't even know if they can get him out.

I'm not sure which is worse, knowing your dad is dead and you'll never see him again or knowing he's alive and you'll never see him again.

I think it's the second one, don't you?

Grandma touches my shoulder and, without saying a word, guides me to our departure gate. I sit and stare off, not looking at anything in particular until the stewardess comes on the loudspeaker.

"We are now boarding flight 2-1-4 for Helsinki with connections to Minsk, Warsaw, and Moscow.

Please have your boarding passes ready as you approach the gate."

I look up at the board that is behind the stewardess at the gate and sure enough, in white letters punched onto a black board are the numbers 214 and the word Helsinki. I look at my grand-mother who is already standing.

"Shall we see what we can do about getting your father out of that prison?" she says as if she is suggesting we are just going to the neighbors to call him home for dinner.

I grasp her hand and blink hard so the tears don't fall out of my eyes as we make our way to the smiling stewardess in the navy-blue Norwegian Air uniform.

A letter from Agnes

Hello again Reader,

Talk about out of the blue! I didn't expect to find out that my dad was still alive, did you? And I also found out that Officer Miller wasn't the bad person he appeared to be. Kind of like Yusuf, if you think about it (though for a much different reason). Out of the blue is another idiom, of course. The idiom dictionary at the DeSoto Public Library explained that it can also be Out of a clear blue sky, which actually gives you more of an idea of the meaning: as if something dropped unexpectedly from the sky. That's exactly how it felt when Officer Miller told us my dad was still alive - it was really, really unexpected information that was just dropped in our laps. But the fact that he is in prison in the Soviet Union (which my teacher, Sister Ann, said is another name for Russia) and that we can't tell Anyone, doesn't help matters much. I don't even think I can tell Peggy. I don't think she'd blab, but what if she talked in her sleep or something. I wouldn't want to put my dad's life — or anyone else's — at risk, like Officer Miller said.

And then there was the expression Grandma used when I was hinting at touring the Royal Palace in Oslo. She told me we have bigger fish to fry. Of course, it doesn't have anything to do with frying fish; it means to have something more important or more interesting to do. And finding out about what happened to my dad was more important, of course.

There are a couple words that weren't defined in the story that are kind of hard, so I thought I'd look them up for you like I did last time, if you haven't already looked them up yourself. The first one is pretense — n: a false reason or explanation that is used to hide the real purpose of something. Grandma asked Mr. Borge to drop the pretense when he was pretending he didn't know my dad had been in Norway. The other word is incarcerated — v: to put (someone — like my dad!) in prison. Though you could probably have figured that one out from what Officer Miller was talking about at the time.

I did liked learning that my dad was working as a pilot for the CIA and that he was helping protect our country, trying to find out what kind of weapons the Russians have (though, of course, Officer Miller couldn't tell me what they had discovered so far).

After I found out about the U2 plane my dad was flying, I asked Officer Miller if we could see it up close. I had seen it from a distance when we had gone to the Norwegian air base with Colonel Wagner, of course, but then I didn't know what it was, and I sure didn't expect that it was the same type of plane my dad had been flying when he got shot down. Now I know what his letter to Grandma Agee meant when he said he was doing something he enjoyed and why he needed safety training. I think the officer felt sorry for us, since he doesn't know if the government can get my dad out of prison, so before he dropped us back off at the hotel, he took us by the air base again so we could see the U2 plane up close.

Officer Miller let me see the <u>sophisticated</u> [adj: <u>highly developed and complex</u>] – the word he used – cameras that are on the plane that allow the pilots to take pictures from so high up. They are really big, and I guess that's how they can see things so far away in such detail. The plane's <u>fuselage</u> [n: <u>the main part of an airplane: the part of an airplane that holds the crew, passengers, and cargo</u>] – another word the officer taught me – was forty feet long with a wing span of eighty feet, which made them sag a bit and why they had supports underneath each wing. Officer Miller said these supports fell off once the plane left the ground. The plane had a clear plastic cover over a lot of the cockpit, where the pilot sat, so Dad must have had a great view from that far up or at least as he was going up or coming down. I don't imagine he saw much down below from 60,000 feet. The cockpit was really small; there was only room for one person to sit and hardly even that for a grown man. The plane was painted a dull black, with no letters or Air Force symbols on it like the other US planes sitting on the tarmac at the air base. I didn't ask but I would guess that's so if anyone saw the plane, they wouldn't know it was one of ours, since it was a spy plane and all. Officer Miller said the long wings (like a glider plane) and the small fuselage (to keep the weight down) helped keep the plane in the air for as long as nine hours, much longer than normal jet airplanes.

Grandma came with, of course, but she seemed preoccupied [adj: thinking about something a lot or too much] with something, looking across the runway at the civilian side of the airport every now and again. I didn't find out until later what she was probably thinking about – Going To Russia!

I can't believe I'm going to Russia! If I thought being in Turkey and Norway was interesting, going to Russia to try and get my dad out of prison is going to be a trip I'll never forget. I'll be sure to take good notes so I can tell you all about it when I get back.

Oh, I almost forgot, I wanted to share the code to the cipher Peggy and I came up with when we were younger. It's kind of silly but

what can you expect from a ten-year-old kid.
Christine (the author) suggested I put it on the
new website she set up for me:

**christinekeleny.wixsite.com/
agneskellymysteries**.

That way you can see all the other cool stuff about
my stories and some hints about what happens on
our trip to Russia.

I'll be in touch.
Your friend (and spy in training!),
Agnes Kelly

Acknowledgment

First I have to thank Petter Snekkestrad of Bodø's Nordlandsmuseet Museum, who found Jan Kristoffer Simonsen, a lifelong resident of Bodø and my Bodø/Norway expert. We struggled a bit with the language difference but with google translate for me and Jan's skill at reading English, we managed. I couldn't have written this book without Jan's help! Audrey Dietrich was kind enough to connect me with a more local Norwegian, her cousin Rønnaug (Hereid) Skindrud. Rønnaug's family moved from Norway in 1957, when she was seven, but she still remembered living there and her parents spoke Norwegian at home. They also ate many of the Norwegian delicacies like laks and lutefisk. Thank you Rønnaug.

And, of course, I need to thank my faithful readers and my new readers: Don Anderson, Mary Behn, Valerie Biel, Andrew Craven, Rachel Craven, Martha Fager, Lorna Lee, Jill Peterson, and Sara Smith.

I have some new student readers this time.

Theresa Smith, a middle school teacher at Belleville Middle School in Wisconsin, found Roxana Grunewald, one of her eighth graders, who was interested in reviewing the story for me. Jill Peterson, a teacher from Raymond School, found three students: Thea Baylor, Norah Beck, and Natalie DeRango. As usual, all my readers gave me great insights and their encouragement is always appreciated.

About the Author

First, I want to thank Agnes for letting me to continue with her story. It was fun to write what happened to Agnes and Grandma in Norway and fun to read it too. If you happened upon this book without reading Agnes' first story: *Intrigue in Istanbul,* you might want to check it out and see where her mystery adventure began.

I've had some middle school classes read Agnes' first story, and it is fun to see what they thought might happen in the second story (this story). Some of them were correct! I'm looking forward to finding out from Agnes what happens on her trip to Russia. I hope she and Grandma are careful!

Along with writing, I run a company called

CKBooks Publishing. I help other people with whatever they need to help them write and eventually publish their own books. It's a fun job for me. If you want to see what I do with my publishing company, you can go to ckbookspublishing.com.

If you want to see all the books I have written so far or if you want to learn a bit more about me, you can go to christinekelenybooks.com. And don't forget to check out Agnes' new website: christinekeleny.wixsite.com/agneskellymysteries.

That's also where I have a Readers' Group sign up, if you want to be one of my special readers.

Thanks for reading Agnes' second story, and I hope you enjoy the third installment in the Agnes Kelly Mystery Adventure Series, as well!

~ Christine

p.s. If you liked this story, please leave a review on your favorite website. Reviews are the lifeblood of all authors (meaning *they are as important to my writing as blood is in our bodies*), especially independently published authors such as myself. ☺

Thank you!